A Trinity Springs Novel: Book One

REBECCA STEVENSON

Copyright © 2022 Rebecca Stevenson

All rights reserved.

Interior formatting by: Dallas Hodge, dalhodge56@gmail.com

Edited by: Michelle Isenhoff, writingupward.com

Cover design by: Valerie Howard
facebook.com/valeriehowardbooks

ISBN: 9798370594229

Dedication

To all American military veterans who have served our country with dignity, honor, and courage. No words could ever thank you enough for your willingness to sacrifice for the common good.

Contents

Chapter One	1
Chapter Two	6
Chapter Three	11
Chapter Four	16
Chapter Five	20
Chapter Six	25
Chapter Seven	31
Chapter Eight	37
Chapter Nine	45
Chapter Ten	52
Chapter Eleven	59
Chapter Twelve	66
Chapter Thirteen	70
Chapter Fourteen	76
Chapter Fifteen	82
Chapter Sixteen	89
Chapter Seventeen	96
Chapter Eighteen	103
Chapter Nineteen	110
Chapter Twenty	115
Chapter Twenty-One	122
Chapter Twenty-Two	129
Chapter Twenty-Three	133
Chapter Twenty-Four	138
Chapter Twenty-Five	144
Chapter Twenty-Six	150
Chapter Twenty-Seven	155

Chapter Twenty-Eight	159
Chapter Twenty-Nine	164
Chapter Thirty	169
Chapter Thirty-One	178
Chapter Thirty-Two	183
Chapter Thirty-Three	191
Chapter Thirty-Four	197
Chapter Thirty-Five	205
Chapter Thirty-Six	212
Chapter Thirty-Seven	217
Chapter Thirty-Eight	223
Chapter Thirty-Nine	230
Chapter Forty	236
Chapter Forty-One	242
Chapter Forty-Two	247
About the Author	255

Chapter One

Lucas Avila discovered his birth certificate in his grandmother's underwear drawer. A newly minted Dallas attorney, he'd come home to Trinity Springs at his aunt's behest to ready the house for sale.

"It's time," Isabel had said. "Mama's been gone almost three months now, but I can't do it. Something happens to me when I touch her clothes. You're going to have to clean everything out and put it on the market."

The white frame house on Bailey Street was in the autumn of its life when Mama Rosa had breathed her last in the tiny bedroom she'd shared with Papa Joe for over fifty years. But the house was full of life when Lucas first knew it—when his mother had dropped him off with a sack of clothes on his third birthday and gone off to God-knows-where.

Mama Rosa and Papa Joe had filled the house with love and laughter during his youth and sent him to college with the money they'd saved for retirement. Now they were both gone, and his childhood home was fraught with memories.

As he unfolded and stared at the yellowed paper, Lucas could almost hear the quiet. He could feel the house of his youth breathing down his neck, its icy breath stirring up ghosts he didn't have time for right now.

A soft knock at the front door jarred him back to the present. He refolded the paper and peered out the front window.

When he opened the door, the young woman took a couple of steps forward and smiled. Waves of dark brown hair cascaded over her shoulders. Her smile lit up her brown eyes. "I heard you were coming back to pack up some things," she said. "Do you remember me?"

No, but I wish I did. Lucas gazed at the beauty in front of him. "Well, I—"

"I'm Maria. I used to live across the street. We played together until my family moved away when I was seven."

Memories of summer evenings flooded his mind. Of a pretty little brown-eyed girl who turned cartwheels on the lawn and caught fireflies in a Mason jar, releasing them at the end of every evening as the grownups dispersed with their folding chairs to their respective houses.

"Why do you do that?" he'd asked one summer night long ago when she twisted open the hole-poked lid and called each by name as one by one they escaped captivity.

"How would you like to spend your life in a jar?"

She had a point.

Lucas managed to jolt himself back to the present. "So it's been what? Twenty years? I'm sorry. Where are my manners? Would you like to come in?" He shoved the folded document into his pants pocket and opened the door wider.

"I don't want to disturb you. I heard you were back in town and thought I'd say hi."

"It's no trouble. I think my aunt left some cake in the kitchen the last time she was here. You could help me remove the temptation."

"I liked your grandmother," Maria said as she entered the living room, leaving behind her the sweet scent of flowers. "I came to see her a few times when she was sick."

"Oh?" Lucas tried to gather his thoughts and focus on the conversation. "That was kind of you to visit her."

"Not really. She cheered me up. Even when she was on hospice and knew she was dying. I saw you at the memorial service. Your eulogy was touching."

"Thanks. Writing the tribute was easy. She was a great lady. So how long have you…"

"Been living here? A few years. My parents rented out the house when they moved to Dallas and then later to the lake. I always loved Bailey Street, so when I started teaching at the elementary school here in Trinity Springs, I figured they might as well rent it to me."

"So you're a teacher?" *Brilliant conversation you're making here, Lucas.* "I guess I'm Captain Obvious since you just said that."

Maria smiled. "Yeah. I'm a music teacher. Kindergarten through fifth grade."

"You're a brave soul."

"I love teaching. I guess it's in my blood. You probably didn't know, but my mama taught in Dallas for fifteen years. She's retired now and my dad works from home, so they decided to settle at Cypress Grove."

Lucas sliced a piece of coconut cake, put it on a plate, and set it, along with a fork and a napkin, in front of Maria. "Coffee? I'll make a fresh pot. Or I think my aunt has some sweet tea in the refrigerator. She whipped up some goodies to entice me to come home and get the house ready to sell."

"You're selling it?" Maria seemed surprised.

"Isabel doesn't want the upkeep of a yard, and I live in Dallas, so…"

"I don't know what I was thinking. Of course you are. I just mean, your family's been here since I can remember. It will be sad to see someone new move in. But I understand."

"My aunt is my only living relative that I know of now, but…" Lucas ran his hand over his left pocket and felt the document he couldn't shrug off, still stunned by the name he'd seen.

"Yes?" Maria prompted him.

"Never mind. I'm not sure what I was going to say. I guess this just isn't home anymore."

"I'll be happy to plant some red begonias out front if you think that will help to sell it," Maria offered. "I'm planting some in my yard too, and I always buy too many."

"Did you plant the flowers last year? I thought my aunt must have done that, but it was you, wasn't it?"

"I remembered flowers in your yard from years ago and thought it might cheer up your grandmother. She was already pretty feeble by then."

"That was thoughtful of you," Lucas said.

Maria carried her empty plate to the sink. "I'd better go and let you get back to whatever you were doing when I interrupted."

"Thank you for the interruption. I was ready for a break. And I'll take you up on the flowers if you were serious."

"Of course. I'll be planting in a few days. It was good to see you again."

"You too… Do you still catch fireflies?"

"You remember that?" she asked with eyes wide.

"That and…didn't we both get bicycles the same Christmas? And your dad taught us to ride them? Mr. Vargas, right?"

"Yeah. I'd forgotten that, but he did. I have fond memories of living here. That's why I wanted to move back after I signed a contract with the school district. I really will get out of your way now, though."

"I'll be here for a week, so I guess I'll see you again?" For an instant he weighed the idea of telling Maria about the discovery of his birth certificate but decided against it. *Don't do anything rash, Lucas. You don't know her well enough to open up your whole life to her.*

"I'll plant the begonias soon," she said. "I'll probably see you then."

Lucas peered out the picture window as Maria proceeded down the front walk, crossed the street, and entered the pale blue frame house, thankful she'd made the effort to be neighborly. He'd have to reciprocate while he was in town.

When she closed her front door, his thoughts returned to a much more pressing matter. He removed the yellowed paper from his pocket and stared again at the name in the box labeled FATHER. What was supposed to have been an uneventful week had already yielded an unexpected visit and an astonishing revelation about his roots.

Chapter Two

Everett Bennington rolled up his sleeping bag and repacked his duffel. It was time to move on. The bridge had served him well for the winter, but spring was tiptoeing in with a promise of warm days followed by triple digits when summer arrived in full force. He'd been a part of Dallas's homeless community long enough to know where to go when the seasons changed.

"Heading out again, Benny?" Paul Carpenter, pastor of Trinity Springs Bible Fellowship an hour north of Dallas, had worked with Everett and his friends for over ten years. He knew very few full names, though. That was their way, remaining anonymous.

"Yup," Everett answered.

"Same place as last year?"

"Yup."

"I'll see you over there then."

"Not if I see you first." It was a joke between the two of them. Paul had started it, and Everett kept it going, chuckling every time one of them said it.

"Take care of yourself."

"Yup." *I wonder what Paul would think if he knew my real name*, Everett thought as he trudged down Cadiz Street laden with all of his earthly possessions. He had traveled this road so many times he could predict to the minute when he would arrive at his destination. And there he would stay until it was time to head back to the bridge in the fall.

It had been a long, cold winter in Dallas, and Everett was grateful for the arrival of spring. Even in the hottest summers, the nights were tolerable, and he could cool off during the day by spending a few hours in the large library downtown. He didn't abuse his privilege, though, the way some of his friends did. They went there to sleep. He went there to read. He'd been known to devour an entire book in one sitting.

Occasionally he would use one of the computers, but mostly he went for the histories and biographies. He figured his parents could have saved a lot of money by turning him loose in a library instead of sending him to SMU. He'd dropped out after his freshman year anyway and joined the army. The year was 1990.

Many of the men and a few of the women in Dallas's homeless community were war veterans. The World War II and Korean War guys were all gone now, but there were still some Vietnam vets and quite a few from the Gulf War. Even more from Afghanistan and Iraq. Everett had enlisted just months before Hussein invaded Kuwait, the event that caused the United States to get involved in Desert Storm.

Everett had always thought his timing unfortunate. Having been born a mere eighteen months after Thomas Bennington, Jr., he'd always been compared to his brother. Thomas was smarter. Thomas was taller and more handsome. Thomas was the athletic one.

He quit striving early on to compete, opting instead to go in a different direction. Whatever Thomas did, Everett would do the opposite, earning him some well-deserved trips to the principal's office at their North Dallas private school and *What were you thinking?* lectures from his parents.

"Benny! Wait up." His buddy Shane, weighted down by his backpack and bedroll, was trotting to catch up with him. Even Shane knew him only by his nickname. And he didn't know Shane's last name. That's the way it was on the street. Anonymity was highly valued.

"'Sup, Shane?"

"Paul and his group serving a meal tonight?"

"Yup."

"You going?"

"Yup."

"That's one cool dude. Why's he do that?" Shane asked.

"Do what?"

"Come down here and bring food. Don't he have a wife and kids? And other things to do 'sides come to this part of town and feed us?"

"He lost a son in Iraq. He knows what we been through," Everett explained.

"You going to the library today?"

"Yup." Everett liked his spring and summer location for a couple of reasons, not the least of which was that it took him only fifteen minutes to walk to the library. He planned to park his belongings and head over there for a few hours of reading before Paul and his team showed up.

"I'll watch your stuff today and go tomorrow," Shane said.

"Thanks. I'll reciprocate then."

"You do like to use them big words."

"That's what they're for. It don't cost any more to use a big word than it does to use a little word." Everett had slipped into street talk—even though he knew better—because he thought it made him seem less pretentious. And the last thing he wanted to do was alienate his friends in the community.

The trek to the Dallas Public Library had become a journey that Everett especially enjoyed in the spring. There was a certain freedom about it when he could doff his coat and leave his belongings behind, looking forward to a few hours of comfort in an overstuffed chair surrounded by a world of information.

His favorite librarian, a wisp of a girl named Hannah—young enough to be his daughter, he thought—had probably saved a new biography or history for him. The thought invigorated him and put a spring in his step. Hannah never treated him disrespectfully as some did. She always called him *sir* and smiled as soon as she saw him get off the elevator and amble toward her desk. Many times she would reach out her hand to shake his, knowing how much he needed a human touch.

One day he'd said to her, "You don't have to call me *sir*. I'm just an old guy who likes to come in out of the heat and read for a while."

"No, sir, you're not," she'd replied. "You put your life on the line when you joined the army. And you went to the Middle East to fight for our country. If that doesn't command my respect, I don't know what does."

"Hi, Benny," she said as soon as she spotted him on her floor. "I put a new book back for you. I knew you'd be coming soon with the weather getting warmer. How was your walk?"

"I saw some daffodils."

"A promise of spring for sure." She reached under her desk and produced the library's newest McCullough. "Have you read this one?"

"No."

"Well, it's yours for the day. And then I'll put it back under my desk until you come in again."

"Day after tomorrow."

"Do you ever read fiction, Benny?"

"Truth is stranger than fiction."

"You probably have a point there," Hannah said, laughing. "I hope you like this one. Follow me."

Hannah made her way to a chair she had piled with books, moved them to a cart she'd parked nearby, and motioned for Everett to sit. He tipped an imaginary hat to her, and she patted his arm. "Enjoy!"

Chapter Three

The three o'clock bell sounded, and Maria Vargas hugged each of her students as they exited the music room. "Have a good weekend, and don't forget to sing."

The kindergartners were her favorites. Blank canvases. She loved introducing them to music appreciation. As she gently laid her guitar in its case, her thoughts focused on what she needed to do before coming back on Monday. Purchasing her spring flowers topped the list. Then there was choir practice Saturday afternoon. And she really needed to squeeze in a visit to her parents. Maybe a little cooking with her mom and fishing with her dad. Would there be time for another visit with her temporary across-the-street neighbor? She hoped so.

She took out her cell and dialed her mother's number as she got in her car. "Hi, Mama. What are you doing?"

"Just put on some chicken to cook for a casserole tonight. Want to join us?"

"Could I take a rain check? I was thinking about going to the garden shop before the selection gets picked over on Saturday. I wondered if you want to join me."

"Oh, honey, I would love to, but I promised your dad an early supper so he can get in some more fishing before dark. You know how picky he is about fishing at dawn and dusk."

"You're a good wife. I'll come out to the lake Sunday afternoon if y'all don't have any plans."

"We don't and that would be nice. Haven't seen you in a couple of weeks."

"These kids keep me hopping... Oh, Mama. Remember that boy I used to play with before we moved to Dallas, Rosa and Joe's grandson? Lucas?"

"Of course I do."

"I talked to him the other day. He's cleaning out the house to sell it. Isabel asked him to help. I actually think he's doing all the work. I haven't seen her car there in several days."

"How's he doing? Where does he live now?"

"He seemed okay...but maybe a little distracted. I think I caught him off guard. I'll fill you in Sunday with what I know, which isn't much. Gotta run now if I'm going to get those flowers. I told him I'd plant some at his house too. Might help it sell."

"I'm blessed to have such a thoughtful daughter. See you Sunday."

"Lemme guess. Your Friday afternoon special? Strawberry lemonade, easy on the ice?" Sherise Washington had started making the drink as soon as she saw Maria park her dark blue Chevy in front of the café.

"Sounds good. Make it to go this time, Sherise. I need to get to the garden shop before it closes."

"You got it," she said as she poured the cold liquid into a plastic cup with a lid. Sherise was old enough to retire, but everyone who knew her knew she never would. She'd owned the café for over thirty years and would probably own it for another ten or twenty if her health held out. Gray peppered her black hair now and there were laugh wrinkles around her dark brown eyes, but she had the energy of a much younger woman.

"Have you been listening to any Paul McCartney or John Lennon today?"

"Are you trying to make me mad, Maria Vargas? I survived the British invasion of the sixties. Just barely, though. Give me some of that Motown any time of the day or night. Diana Ross...now that girl could sing."

"Can't disagree with you on that. What about Smokey Robinson?"

"Ooowee yes! Him too. Love me some Motown. You got your guitar in the car?"

"I do," Maria said. "But I'll have to play for you some other time. Buying flowers for my house and Rosa's today."

"I hear Lucas is back in town. You seen him?"

"Yeah. I went over the other day. I don't think he remembered me at first. I was seven when we left for Dallas, and I hadn't seen him since I moved back." Maria took a sip of her drink. "You still make the best strawberry lemonade in town, Sherise."

"I make the *only* strawberry lemonade in town, girl, and don't you forget it."

"I won't." She smiled. "See you at choir practice tomorrow?"

"I'll be there with bells on. If you see Lucas again, tell him to come see his old friend Sherise. He used to do his homework at that table over there in the corner. He's done gone and become a fancy big-city, hot-shot lawyer, but he needs to remember his roots. And his roots are right here in Trinity Springs. When he gets to the Supreme Court, I'm gonna close that table and put his name on it."

Maria laughed, but as she walked to her car, her thoughts returned to that "big-city, hot-shot lawyer" who had just re-entered her life. She'd thought of him many times while she was living in Dallas…and especially after moving back here to their old neighborhood in Trinity Springs. Rosa had spoken of him a few times, but Maria hadn't wanted to ask. She knew he'd become an attorney and lived in Dallas, but that was about as far as their conversations had gone.

The question of his birth parents had never come up. As far as Rosa had been concerned, Lucas was her boy and she was proud of him.

"Hi, Walter!" Maria shouted across the rows of dwarf yaupons and holly ferns at Green Thumb Garden Shop to the man in overalls and straw hat.

"Well, there she is! I figured you'd be coming to see me soon. What'll it be this time? Begonias or impatiens?"

"I'm going with those scarlet begonias again this year, Walter. And I'll need enough for Rosa's house. I told Lucas I'd plant some there too."

"I heard Rosa's boy was back in town. You seen him? How's he look? I haven't laid eyes on that boy in years."

"He looks like he did when we were kids," Maria said, "only twenty years older if you can picture that."

"Oh, I saw him plenty around town till he went off to college. Mostly at Sherise's. I think she helped raise that boy. I guess you know the story about his mother dropping him off with Rosa and Joe and then just disappearing."

"He seems to be doing well now."

"So you're planting flowers for him, are ya?" Walter raised his eyebrows.

"I'm doing it for Rosa. She loved flowers so much."

"Umm hmm…" he said, rolling his eyes and putting six flats of begonias on the cart for her. "Is that gonna be enough for both yards?"

"I think so. If I need more, I know where you are."

Chapter Four

"Everett Bennington. I wonder if he's one of the wealthy Dallas Benningtons. If he is... I mean, man... you've got it made for life." Lucas was on the phone with Cooper MacDonald, his law school friend and now colleague at Benson and Hughes Law Firm, and had just told him about the name on his birth certificate.

"Don't go there, Coop. I don't know what I'm going to do with this information...if anything. I could be opening up a huge can of worms."

"If I were you, I'd start with social media. If you can't find him there, that might mean he doesn't want to be found...for whatever reason."

"What do you know about the Benningtons?" Lucas put his cell phone on speaker, laid it on the kitchen table, and continued cleaning the pantry. "I've heard of them, but that's about all. You've lived in Dallas all your life, so I'm sure you know more than I do."

"I think he made his money in oil. And his wife is this big Dallas socialite who's always throwing extravagant parties. What if they're your grandparents? Oh, man!"

"I'd say that's doubtful. My mother's name is Carmen Avila. Sound like she'd have a relationship with someone like that? You knew my grandparents. Greatest people in the world, but socialites they were not. And they never lived in Dallas as far as I know. Now I wish I'd asked more questions. Well, it's too late now."

"What about your aunt?"

"Isabel was thirteen when I was born. Teenagers are usually in their own tunnel-vision world," Lucas said. "So I doubt she'd know anything."

"How's the house cleanout coming?"

"Slowly. Had an unexpected visitor yesterday. She lives across the street. A girl who lived there until her parents moved when we were both seven. She's back now and teaches music at the elementary school in Trinity Springs."

"Apparently she remembered you. Did you remember her?"

"It came back to me gradually."

"Married?"

Lucas had to laugh at his friend. Cooper always got right to the point, and when it came to a pretty girl, that was always the point. "I didn't ask, but she wasn't wearing a ring."

"So you looked."

"Well…"

"Hot?"

"You could say that. In fact, you *would* say that."

"Well, if you're not interested, send her my way."

"Right now all I'm interested in is getting this house cleaned out and selling it. Isabel lives in an apartment and doesn't want to deal with the yard at the house anymore. Speaking of yard, Maria volunteered to plant some begonias in the front flower bed to help it sell."

"Hmmm…"

"She's probably right," Lucas conceded, "and this is the perfect time to put a house on the market...or so I hear."

"Too bad it's such a long commute. You could live there and be across the street from a hot, single—"

As if his friend could see him, Lucas rolled his eyes and shook his head. "I wish I hadn't mentioned her. I'll never hear the end of it now."

"Gotta run. Let me know if I can help with anything."

"Thanks, Coop. See you in the office in a few days."

Lucas put his phone back in his pants pocket and examined the birth certificate again...for about the thousandth time, he thought. It just didn't add up. Everett Bennington would have been the very last name he would've picked from a list of potential fathers. In a way, he was surprised his mother had listed him. For what purpose? Was she expecting to see him again? To talk him into marriage? Lucas knew so little about his early years. His life essentially began when he went to live with his grandparents. They became parents to him and rarely talked about the three years he lived with his mother.

They told him once about the day he was born. It had been an unusually cold day in September when his mom went into labor and they rushed her to the community hospital. She'd delivered a healthy baby boy and brought him home the next day. Within six months, she'd moved in with a friend who lived in Dallas, and Joe and Rosa hadn't seen Lucas much after that. Until the day Carmen dropped him at their house and took off. She wouldn't tell them where she was going—just that she couldn't do it anymore. Couldn't work and take care of a kid too.

Lucas never got the feeling from his grandparents that they resented being saddled with a three-year-old. In fact, they treated him like the son they'd never had. He realized years later they did without so they could give him a good life. He received grants and scholarships, but they footed the bill for the rest of college. He worked the year after college to save money for law school, but they helped him with what little savings they had. As a result, he had very few school loans to pay off. And for that he had Mama Rosa and Papa Joe to thank.

Chapter Five

At half past seven on Saturday morning, Lucas was awakened by barking dogs and got up to peer out the window of his front bedroom. Red flowers lined both sides of the walkway from the street to the front door, and Maria was gathering her spade, the empty containers, and leftover potting soil. How long, he wondered, had she been working? It was barely morning. He threw on jeans and a T-shirt and went outside.

"Hey!" he said, running his fingers through his unruly hair. "Looks great. I didn't know you were going to plant that many."

"I always get carried away when I go to the garden shop, and they'd just received a new shipment when I got there yesterday."

"Thanks for doing this. I'll pay you for the flowers."

Maria shook her head. "No you won't. I'm doing this to honor Rosa's memory. She was a special lady who loved flowers as much as I do."

"You're right about that. I wish I'd done more for her and Papa while they were alive."

"They were so proud of you. You should have no regrets. I'm almost done here, and I'll get out of your way. I hope I didn't wake you."

"Have you had breakfast?" Lucas mentally crossed his fingers, hoping she hadn't. "I make a pretty mean omelet."

"No, but I don't want to hold you up if you have other things to do."

"I don't. Let me pay you back in a very small way for the flowers...with breakfast."

"Okay. Sounds good. Let me go home to wash up. I'll just be a minute." She picked up her box of planting tools and headed across the street.

Lucas was surprised but pleased when Maria returned in what seemed like an extremely short time, considering she had changed from her yard-work clothes into a lime green sundress. She looked really good this early in the morning with her dark brown hair falling just below her shoulders in waves. Her face appeared freshly washed, and she had on just the slightest hint of lipstick. He found her stunning and had to will himself to look away and tend to the omelet in the skillet.

"How can I help?" she asked.

"Want to pour two glasses of juice? Or there's fresh coffee if you want a cup."

"Juice is fine. Those omelets smell so good. I guess I worked up an appetite and didn't realize it. Do you cook a lot?"

"I have my specialties." Lucas flipped an omelet. "Not many, though. You?"

"Same. I make a few of my mama's recipes. That reminds me. I was in Sherise's yesterday, and she wants you to come see her while you're in town. Said something about a special table where you used to do your homework."

His mind journeyed to afternoons spent at that table with Sherise, the ever-willing tutor, there to help when he got stuck on something. If she couldn't help him work a math problem or diagram a sentence, she would take his mind off it for a while and ease his anxiety. And sometimes the answer would come then.

He couldn't begin to count how many cups of hot chocolate and glasses of strawberry lemonade he'd consumed sitting in the corner of that café. Sherise wasn't able to have children of her own and her husband died young, Lucas's grandmother had told him, so she considered her special customers as family. He knew he had been blessed to have her in his life.

"I do need to see her soon. She probably helped me through school as much as any of my teachers. Did you know she's a history buff?"

"You mean in areas other than music? She certainly knows a lot of music history."

"Oh yeah. She reads all the time. Totally self-educated. She didn't get to go to college, and I'm not sure she finished high school. She had to take care of her siblings after her stepmom died."

"So they were her half brothers and sisters?"

"Yes. Her mom died when she was five," Lucas explained, "and her dad remarried a year later. But she always says, 'There are no fractions in our family.' I'll go by for lunch today. Want to join me?"

"I'd better not. I still have to plant the begonias in my yard and get the music ready for choir practice this afternoon. I'm going to the lake to see my parents tomorrow afternoon. Would you like to go? If you enjoy fishing, my dad would be delighted to hook you up with a rod and reel and some of his special lures."

"Well…" Thoughts of the many things he had to do to clean out the house flitted across his mind.

"Don't feel obligated. I know you're busy here. I just thought you might want to escape the packing for a while.

I'm sure they'd love to see you after all these years. They asked me how you were doing."

"Let me see how much I can get done today. Can I let you know later?"

"Of course. Want me to put my number in your phone?"

Smart move, Lucas. Getting a girl's number had never been so easy.

Lucas sorted and packed swiftly and efficiently for three hours after Maria left. Nothing like a pretty girl and a potential visit to an old friend for incentive. His plan was to surprise Sherise at lunchtime and then call Maria and take her up on her offer to go to the lake. He'd never been much of a fisherman, but it would be good to see the Vargases again. He remembered their kindness from so many years ago.

All the while the birth certificate lay in the back of his mind. And every so often it would float to the forefront and completely occupy his thoughts. He had so many questions. Did this Everett Bennington, whoever he was, know his name was on this newly discovered piece of paper? Did he know he had a son who'd become a lawyer and lived in Dallas now? How had he met Lucas's mother? Was he still in touch with her? Where did he live? What did he do? Did he have any other children? The thought that he might have brothers and sisters hadn't occurred to Lucas until that minute, and he wondered how he could find out.

Cooper had mentioned social media, so he took his phone out of his pocket and searched the four sites that immediately came to mind. He saw very few Everett Benningtons, and none who would be the right age. Chances were his father, for whatever reason, didn't want to be found.

But what about the other Benningtons Coop had mentioned? He needed first names, so he went to his preferred search engine and typed in "Bennington" and "Dallas" and "oil and gas." Bingo! Thomas Bennington, Sr. and Thomas Bennington, Jr. popped up.

The article led him to a Sally Bennington, member of Dallas's Junior League. That sounded right, judging by what Cooper said about the wife being a socialite. There was also a Keri Bennington, wife of the son. But no mention of an Everett Bennington. Surely there was a better way to search.

He'd thought of mentioning the birth certificate to Maria since she and her parents had lived in Dallas for several years. He wasn't sure how much he wanted to share with people he didn't know well, though…hadn't seen in twenty years.

His growling stomach told him it was time to head to Sherise's. He hadn't eaten a really good meal since he'd arrived in Trinity Springs, but he could get one at the café. If she still had the same head cook she'd employed for as long as he could remember, it would taste spectacular. He knew the menu by heart and began to run through it in his mind. Chicken and dumplings, the kind Mama Rosa used to make, won…with a plate of meatloaf and mashed potatoes to go. Might as well have something on hand for tomorrow.

Chapter Six

Trinity Springs was one of those small Texas towns where folks still waved at passing cars and shouted *Howdy!* as they strolled by neighbors sitting on front porch swings in the evening. A small town large enough that you didn't know everybody…but just about. Not far enough west to be full of cactuses and tumbleweeds and not far enough east to be full of pine trees and azaleas. But with field after field of bluebonnets and Indian paintbrush in the spring and spectacular crimson and gold sunsets year-round. And with a recently renovated quintessential town square built around a limestone courthouse to rival any.

Sherise's Café sat on the southeast corner of that town square as it had for fifty plus years. Until 1992, it had been known only as the Trinity Springs Café, but when Sherise Washington purchased it, she personalized the name along with the menu and the service. She greeted most of her customers by name and remembered many of their favorite foods.

She was known around town as *The Hugger*, so if you needed a hug or a good old-fashioned meal with lots of comfort food and fresh vegetables, Sherise's was the place to go.

"Get over here and give your old friend a hug," Sherise said as she threw her thin velvet-brown arms around Lucas. She'd always given the best hugs, he thought as he gave her a kiss on the cheek. The smell of lavender, her signature scent, mingled with the aroma of baked goods and reminded him how fortunate he was that this café had been his home-away-from-home for as long as he could remember.

"Ooowee, I have missed you! You haven't been in here since you came home for Rosa's service, have you?"

"No, ma'am, I haven't."

"That's too long." She eyed him over her spectacles.

"Yes, ma'am, it is." *Way to lay a guilt trip on me*, he chuckled to himself.

"Come. Let's sit at your table. Tina, bring a menu and two strawberry lemonades. Anything else before you order? Chips and salsa?"

"No, thanks. I already know what I want without looking at a menu." Neither the menu nor the décor at Sherise's Café had changed since Lucas could remember, but he supposed people liked it that way. Dark plank floors that creaked just the right amount as customers strolled from the door to their favorite booth or table. Plastic blue and white checked tablecloths that could be easily wiped clean after each use. Booths and chairs with just enough padding to encourage people to sit and visit a while. No, he couldn't imagine that anyone would want Sherise to make any changes…and she hadn't.

"Good. You can tell Tina when she brings the drinks. How are you? Getting everything cleaned out? Is it hard? That's a silly question," Sherise said, admonishing herself. "I know it is. It's never easy selling your childhood home. I started to do it after my daddy passed, but I couldn't part with it."

"It's lovely. I'm glad you kept it. How are your brother and sisters?" Lucas asked.

"Fit as a fiddle. All moved away, so I don't see them often. We FaceTime, though. Are you impressed? Sherise is a techie." She threw her head back and laughed.

"Impressed, but not surprised. Sherise can do anything she sets her mind to. I've known that since I was in first grade and Mama Rosa dropped me off at this table for the first time."

"I was your official, unofficial babysitter, tutor, nanny, and governess for most of your growing up years, you might say."

"I *would* say, and I'm blessed to be able to say that. I couldn't have had a better teacher."

"Thanks, Tina," Sherise said as the server set the drinks and a menu in front of them.

"Good to see you, Lucas. What'll it be today?" Tina removed the pencil that was always stuck in the bun on the back of her head.

Lucas looked up at the woman who'd worked at Sherise's for as long as he'd been going there. "Hi, Tina. I'd like chicken and dumplings for lunch and a plate of meatloaf and mashed potatoes to go."

"Vegetables? Creamed corn, black-eyed peas, collard greens?"

"Surprise me."

"Can do. I know what you like. You haven't been away *that* long," Tina said over her shoulder as she headed for the kitchen.

Sherise was the one remaining person in Lucas's life besides Cooper that he felt comfortable opening up to, and he decided to put all his cards on the table. "I found my birth certificate, Sherise."

Her dark brown eyes widened. "Did you now?"

"I think Mama Rosa tried to hide it but forgot about it when she realized she was dying. Either that or she thought it was time I knew and wanted me to find it."

"Time you knew what? You knew your mama's name all along, didn't you?"

"Did you know my father?"

"Your *father*? I have no idea. Your mother never said that I know of, and I never heard it from Joe or Rosa either. That is, if they knew."

"They knew. It's on the birth certificate." He took the paper out of his pocket, unfolded it, and laid it on the table in front of his friend.

"Ooowee! Now that's a name! And not one I would have expected."

"Do you know him?"

"No. It's just an interesting sounding name, that's all. Do you?"

"No."

"Do you want to?" she asked.

"I'm not sure," Lucas admitted. "What do you think?"

"This is one of those times I wish I had a crystal ball."

"I'm curious, of course. But I don't know, Sherise. I don't want to be disappointed and that could happen. I just have to decide which one outweighs the other—curiosity or fear of disappointment. My friend Cooper knows of some Benningtons in Dallas. Said they're pretty rich and high up on the social ladder. Made their money in oil. I don't think the daughter of Joe and Rosa Avila would have had a relationship with someone in that family."

"Well, now wait a minute. Don't dismiss that possibility completely. Do you want me to tell you what I know…or would you rather leave it alone?"

"You know something?" Lucas leaned in.

"Don't know if it's relevant, but your mother was living and working in Dallas when she got pregnant with you. Came back to Trinity Springs when she started showing.

She was cleaning houses down there. Make more sense as a possibility now?"

Lucas stared out the window, as if something outside the café would make this make sense. "I don't think I can let this go. I could have a family out there somewhere. It might not be a family I'd want, but I have to find out. What would you do in my place?"

"You know me," Sherise said. "Curiosity is a huge force in my life."

"I guess I got that from you…by osmosis rather than inheritance." He smiled and Sherise patted his hand.

"You seen that pretty neighbor of yours since you been back?"

"I assume you're talking about Maria Vargas…and I'd be surprised if you didn't already know I've seen her."

"Well…maybe I do and maybe I don't."

"My money's on *do*. But, yes, a couple of times, in fact. She invited me to go to the lake with her tomorrow afternoon to see her parents. It's been so long, but I remember them a little bit."

"They lived in Dallas for several years, you know. Might've heard of some Benningtons. Worth asking, I'd say. Whew! What a name!"

"I don't know if I'm ready to get other people mixed up in this yet. Especially people I don't know well."

"They're good people, Lucas. Maria's an angel. What she's done for some of those kids in her classes with music is pretty amazing. That reminds me. I'm going to choir practice at three. She leads the choir and might fuss at me if I'm late, so I'd better wrap things up here. I'll go and let you eat. Tina will bring that meatloaf when you get ready to leave."

"Thanks, Sherise. I'm glad I still have you. Gives me some roots here."

Sherise rose and patted her protégé on the shoulder. "Don't stay away so long next time."

When he'd polished off his meal, Lucas texted Maria.

If the offer still stands, I'd like to go with you to the lake tomorrow.

She texted back immediately.

I'll pick you up at 3:00 if that's okay. I don't plan to stay late, but we'll have supper over there. Mama's making a big batch of tamales.

Lucas replied.

Sounds good. I'm looking forward to seeing them again.

Chapter Seven

Lucas had worked all Sunday morning, digging up memory after memory as he packed away his childhood home and tossed items he felt no one would want. The process should have been cathartic, but instead it was becoming dreary and draining, and he was beginning to understand his aunt's refusal to take on the task.

For as long as he could remember, he'd been sure Isabel resented him. Because she hadn't tried to hide her jealousy, he suspected she thought her parents were disappointed their second child wasn't the boy they'd been hoping for, and when Lucas arrived, their wish had been granted in an unconventional way. It was just a theory, but to him it made perfect sense and explained why his aunt had always ignored him.

At one time he'd suspected she resented his college education, but in time he'd come to realize she hadn't wanted to go to college. She might have begrudged the money her parents spent on his degrees, but she'd never voiced that sentiment…to Lucas anyway. Instead, she'd taken a job right out of high school at a factory on the outskirts of town and rented a studio apartment above a friend's garage. She seemed content. Aloof, but content.

Lucas's phone vibrated on the table. "Hey, Coop. What's up?"

"I just talked to my mom. She's pretty in touch with Dallas society, and she actually knows quite a bit about the Benningtons. And get this. She said they had another son besides Thomas Bennington, Jr. She didn't know his name. Said he just seemed to vanish several years ago."

"Really?" Lucas dropped an armload of clothes on the bed and plopped down in a chair in the corner of the room.

"Yeah. I've been trying to find his name, but I've run into a brick wall. It appears he doesn't want to be found."

"I guess I shouldn't pursue this…but, on the other hand, my father's out there somewhere, and I have a name for him…so…"

"I think you're going to have to talk to Thomas Bennington. If Everett Bennington isn't his long-lost son, he might be a nephew or something. And if not, at least you will have ruled that out. Then you can try another angle."

"What other angle?" *Because I certainly can't think of one.*

Cooper laughed. "I have no idea. Just wanted to pass that on to you…for what it's worth."

"I appreciate the info. Not sure what it's worth yet, but it kind of spurs me on to take the next step."

"Which is?"

"You were right. I have to talk to Thomas Bennington, Sr. I have to start there. I'm not sure he'll see me. I might have to play the lawyer card."

"Let me know if you need top-notch representation. I'll give you the friends and family discount."

"You might be interested to know I'm going to see my hot neighbor's parents this afternoon. They live at the lake just outside of town, and she invited me to go with her."

"Just a reminder that I would make one heck of a best man."

"Noted. Gotta run. We're leaving at three."

"Keep me posted on the Bennington thing. I'm holding down the fort at the office, but it'll be good to have you back."

"You know I've been working from here, right? John has been sending me documents to go over on the FennCom account."

"Yeah, but I've missed our lunches. Craving some barbecue at Sol's."

"You should come up here sometime. My friend Sherise owns a café on the square and the food's great."

"Maybe I will. Have fun with the hot neighbor."

"You're a little dressed up for fishing," Maria said when Lucas responded to her light knock and opened the door. Although she liked what she saw. Light tan chinos with a brown and navy plaid short-sleeved shirt. He was once again that seven-year-old boy she'd had a crush on so many years ago. But this time that boy was all grown up and more good-looking than ever. She willed her eyes away from his brown ones and walked in. "Why don't you throw a pair of jeans and a T-shirt in a bag just in case. I doubt my dad will let you get away with sitting on the dock. He'll talk you into going out in the boat for some largemouth bass fun. At least *he'll* think it's fun."

"Will do. I'm not much of a fisherman, but I guess if he can teach me to ride a bike, he can teach me to fish."

"Do you mind if I drive?" Maria asked when he returned to the living room with a small bag. "I can practically set my car on autopilot."

"Sure. No problem. You're lucky your parents live so close. Do you see them often?" Lucas asked as he locked the front door.

"Usually every weekend, but sometimes I get busy and don't see them for two weeks."

The ride to Cypress Grove Lake took thirty minutes, but Maria found herself wishing it was longer. She wanted to get to know Lucas again, as an adult this time. Wanted to know if he was still that same innocent, fun-loving little boy she remembered playing with. Or had time and law school and living in Dallas changed him? She was aware of what a big city could do to a person, and that was one reason she had come back to Trinity Springs as soon as there was a job opening at the local elementary school.

It was already warm, warmer than normal for this time of year, so Maria had the air conditioner on. Normally she would have turned the radio on too, but today she wanted to spend quality time with her former neighbor. He'd seemed to have something on his mind—something bothering him—both times she'd talked with him, and she was determined to find out what it was.

He interrupted her thoughts. "I can't remember the last time I went to Cypress Grove Lake. Maybe it was when I was in high school. Mama Rosa and Papa Joe took me, but we didn't fish. We picnicked. Thank you for inviting me today. I need to get back to my roots."

"Everybody does. I guess my roots should be in Dallas since I lived there most of my life, but I don't feel that way. I never got Trinity Springs out of my mind. Or out of my heart. I don't think my parents did either, since they came back up here as soon as they could."

More silence followed, but not an awkward silence. Maria always enjoyed the bucolic fields and meadows that lay between Trinity Springs and Cypress Grove. Lucas seemed content staring out at the rural scenery too. Fields dotted with cows and horses. Miles of whitewashed wood fences. The earliest pink and yellow wildflowers beginning to bloom.

After a few more minutes, she broke the silence. "Tell me about your life in Dallas. Where do you work and live? Are you happy there?"

"Happy? I'm not unhappy that I went to law school, but sometimes I wish I could do something more…I don't know…fulfilling maybe. Rewarding? There's often a dirty underbelly to corporate law. But maybe that's just life in general, and I didn't realize it until I was an adult and on my own. I suppose I had a pretty sheltered childhood in Trinity Springs. I'm sure my grandparents had problems I knew nothing about."

"Don't you think that's true of all households, all families? No family is perfect, and I think most parents try to protect their kids by keeping them in the dark, so to speak, about some things."

"Probably. But to answer your question about where I work and live…North Dallas. My office is off the Dallas Tollway, and my apartment is about ten minutes up the road. I work with a good friend I met in law school, Cooper MacDonald. He's a great guy. Maybe you'll meet him soon. I'm trying to get him to come to Trinity Springs so I can introduce him to Sherise. And now, you too."

"I'd love to meet him. I work with my best friend too."

"Is she from Trinity Springs? Would I know her?"

"I doubt it. She grew up on their ranch right outside Trinity Springs, but she was homeschooled, so you wouldn't have known her from school. Her name's Kacie Griffin."

"Doesn't ring a bell," he said.

Maria turned down a dirt road lined with overhanging trees on both sides, and Lucas rolled down his window to smell the air. "Ah. This is nice. Fresh country air. Brings back good memories."

"I love to come out here on weekends. Clears the cobwebs from the week."

"I didn't know you got cobwebs. You love teaching, right?"

"I love being in the classroom, yes. Some other things aren't so pleasant. Like staff meetings and bureaucracy. Politics."

"Politics? Seriously?"

"Yes, we have politics even in small school districts like Trinity Springs. I try to steer clear of that stuff. Fortunately, I'm the only music teacher at my school, so I don't have to try to coordinate with other teachers. I hear about problems, though."

"It's a good thing you're not in the corporate world."

"For many reasons…" Maria turned off the road and pulled her car into the gravel driveway of a pale yellow frame cottage surrounded by oak and cypress trees. "We're here."

Chapter Eight

As Lucas stepped out of the car, he heard country music coming through the open front door. Mrs. Vargas breezed out onto the porch, banging the screen door behind her. "Welcome! Y'all come on in! My, my! Lucas Avila. You've not only grown up, but you're better-looking now than when you were a cute little boy!"

"Mama! Don't embarrass him first thing," Maria admonished.

"Don't try to tell me you don't agree, daughter of mine."

"Don't embarrass me too," Maria said, laughing.

"Well, Lucas," her mother continued undeterred, "you grew up to be a mighty fine-looking young man."

"Thank you, ma'am."

"And manners, too. I'm not surprised. Rosa wouldn't have had it any other way, I'm sure."

"No, ma'am. She wouldn't."

"I'm sorry we missed her service, but we were out of town that week. I heard it was lovely, though… Well, why are we standing here? Come on in the kitchen. That's where all the action is. Let me turn this music down. I would turn it off, but my music-loving family would overrule me."

"That's okay, Mama. You can turn it off while we have company, as far as I'm concerned."

She reached over, clicked off the Bluetooth speaker, and paused the station on her phone.

"Hey! What happened to the music?" a male voice called from the back porch.

"Come in, Daddy," Maria said. "We have company."

"Well, well, well. If it isn't the little Avila boy all grown up now. How are you, son?" He reached out his big, not-so-clean hand toward Lucas, after he'd swiped it slightly across his jeans. "Excuse my unsanitary handshake. I've been cleaning fish for this little lady." He leaned over and gave his wife a peck on the cheek. "Caught a nice mess of 'em this morning. Don't worry, though," he said to Lucas. "There's more where those came from. You might dirty up those nice clothes a little though."

Lucas smiled at Maria. "I have some other clothes in the car, Mr. Vargas. Maria said we might go fishing. I look forward to it."

"Let the children sit down, Rob. You can stay out of the lake a little while longer, can't you? Your daughter just got here."

"Sure I can." He threw his massive arms around Maria and gave her a long hug.

Lucas wasn't sure what he'd expected, but the Vargases were what many people would refer to as down-to-earth. Good folks. Country folks. Not what he was used to anymore—and he'd missed it after moving to Dallas—but he liked them immediately.

"I made some *queso blanco*, Lucas. Would you like some? We'll eat supper around five. Then I'm sure Rob will want to introduce you to our lake."

"Yes, ma'am. That sounds good, Mrs. Vargas."

"You're all grown up now," she said as she dipped up four small bowls of *queso* and put some blue corn chips on the table with them. "Do you think you could call us Livvy and Rob?"

"Of course. It seems strange in a way...seeing you after so many years. But in another way, it doesn't seem like any time at all has passed."

"We had some good times in that neighborhood, didn't we, Rob?" Livvy said.

"Sure did. Your granddaddy was a fine man, Lucas," Rob said. "Your grandmamma was a fine woman too, but I knew Joe better. We used to borrow each other's tools. And sometimes we teamed up to work on honey-do's...if you know what I mean. When you get married, your wife says, 'Honey, do this. Honey, do that.' That's the way they think they can keep you out of trouble, but sometimes it just gets you in more trouble. Remember that, son. That little tidbit might come in handy one of these days."

"Yes, sir," Lucas agreed, laughing. "I can imagine that's true."

"Maria, why don't you show Lucas around the property while Daddy finishes cleaning the fish and I put the finishing touches on the tamales and salad," Livvy suggested after they had chatted and snacked on queso and chips for a while.

"How about a grand tour, Lucas?" Maria threw a knowing sideways glance at her mother.

"Sure. I'd like that." He rose and followed Maria out the back door, past her dad's fish-cleaning station on the screened-in back porch, thinking to himself how glad he was Rob hadn't invited him to help with *that* task.

"There really isn't much to see out here. I think Mama just wanted us out of the kitchen so she could concentrate on her tamales," Maria said.

"This is nice, though. So peaceful. I'm sure they like living here…as opposed to Dallas, I mean.

"Dallas was good in many ways. I think we were just tired of it. The traffic mostly. Daddy wasn't able to work from home then, and he hated the commute."

"What does he do?" Lucas asked.

"He does IT consulting. Contract work. He doesn't get one gig finished before he's signing up for another one. He doesn't advertise. Just word-of-mouth because he's really good at what he does."

"You're very close to your parents, aren't you?"

"Yes. Maybe because I grew up as an only child. I don't know. I had an older brother who would've been two when I was born, but he lived only a few hours after a very difficult birth."

"I'm so sorry to hear about that, Maria. Mama Rosa never mentioned it."

"It hit my parents really hard, as you would expect, and they don't talk about it much. We visit his gravesite on his birthday every year."

They meandered over to a raised and tilled bed that Lucas supposed was going to be a vegetable garden in a couple of months.

"This is my daddy's garden," Maria explained. "His other hobby besides fishing. He'll plant a few vegetables in a week or two."

"And he's still working full-time. He stays busy, doesn't he?"

"Yes, and it makes Mama happy. She can enjoy her two hobbies in peace and quiet—cooking and reading."

"Do you have any hobbies?"

"You mean besides music?"

"Well, yeah…"

"I like to read too. And flowers. I guess I got my love of the outdoors from Daddy."

"Reading? Really? Maybe some day we can compare notes on books."

"I'd like that. How long will you be in Trinity Springs?" Maria asked.

"I'm afraid it's going to take longer than I originally anticipated to get the whole house cleaned out and ready to sell. One week won't cut it. I don't know what I was thinking. I need to go back into the office soon, but I'll be back on weekends for a while."

Lucas liked the smile that appeared on Maria's face. They continued in silence down to the lake. A canoe and a flat-bottom fishing boat drifted by as they stood drinking in the quiet. "Motorboats aren't allowed on Cypress Grove, and that was the main appeal of the lake to them," Maria said. "That, and the sunsets each evening when cloud formations happen to be just right."

"I can see why they wanted to settle here," Lucas said. "It's a far cry from anything they could have found in Dallas."

"And for half the cost of buying there. They looked, but I think they always knew they'd end up back here."

Lucas and Maria wandered back up to the house and checked in with Rob. "Your mother just told me to get washed up for supper. Want to see if she needs any help?"

"Sure."

"Anything I can do?" Lucas asked.

"I'll find a job for you," Maria said. "Don't worry."

"You ready to find your new happy place, son?" Rob asked after the tamales, salad, and apricot fried pies had been devoured and Lucas had changed into jeans and a T-shirt.

"Yes, sir."

"Then what are we waiting for? If we stay around here any longer they'll expect us to help with the kitchen cleanup."

"I'll be happy to help and then go fishing," Lucas offered. "That was a fine meal, Livvy. Best tamales I've had in a very long time."

"Don't be silly," Livvy said, laughing. "Maria and I can do this a lot faster if you guys are on the lake. Thanks for offering, though. And I'm glad you enjoyed the tamales."

"Don't keep him out too long," Maria called to her father. "I have some lesson plans to write when I get home."

"The fish will determine that," Rob replied, grabbing his tackle box and two rods and reels. "Come on, son. Don't mind them. We guys have to do what we have to do."

"Yes, sir. That sounds like something Papa Joe would have said." Lucas followed Rob on the twisting path down to the lake where the twelve-foot, flat-bottom boat awaited them.

"Yep. He had a good head on his shoulders, he did. I gained a lot of wisdom from your grandpa. Admired the way he respected and loved your grandmother. I guess I might even have tried to emulate him a little bit. Here. Step over this way into the boat." Rob gave it a gentle push just before getting in himself.

"Grab a paddle, son. We're going over to that group of cypress stumps on your left. The fish usually huddle over there at dusk. Slow and easy. Don't want to spook them… Have you ever cast?"

"No, sir."

They paddled for a few quiet minutes before Rob asked, "Are you right-handed?"

"Yes, sir."

"So am I. I like to cast with my left hand so I can reel with my right. But some folks like to cast with their right hand and then switch hands. That's too much rigmarole for me. Why don't you try it my way first?"

"Okay… Like this?" Lucas held the rod in his left hand, keeping his thumb on the reel, and pretended to cast toward the stumps as a slight breeze stirred the cypress branches.

"That's the way. Now release when you cast. Not too far, though. You don't want to get hung up on the trees... Good one. Are you sure you haven't done this before?"

"No, sir, I haven't. But when Maria told me we would probably go fishing, I watched a couple of videos. Is that cheating?"

Rob reared his head back and laughed a hearty laugh. "That, my boy, is what I call preparation, not cheating. Have another go at it. There should be some fish right where you put in last time."

Lucas cast his lure where the fish were supposed to be. "Uh... Rob." His voice raised in intensity. "Uh... I think I might have something."

"Reel it in, boy...but not too fast. Take it slow and easy... Pull it up... Well, would you look at that?" Rob said as Lucas pulled up a medium-sized, largemouth bass. "Livvy's gonna enjoy cooking that one. Might have him for breakfast. Unless you want us to save him for you."

"No, sir. You enjoy him. Maybe I'll come back sometime and catch another one."

"You're welcome here anytime, son. I've been needing a fishing partner. Maria goes out with me sometimes, but Livvy has no interest in it. She can cook 'em up mighty delicious, though."

"I'll bet she can!"

"Here. I'll take him off and put him right here in the ice chest. Maria said you live in Dallas now."

"Yes, sir."

"Do you like it?"

"It's not Trinity Springs, but the opportunities for lawyers outweigh those here."

"We lived there for almost twenty years, you know. I never really took to it, but, as you say, that's where the work was. Too much concrete for me. Dallas has streets named for trees they cut down to make the streets. Oak. Elm. Go figure."

They stayed on the lake about thirty minutes longer, and Rob caught a couple more. Then he said, "I guess we'd better mosey on back to the house. My daughter said not to keep you out too late."

"I've really enjoyed it, though. Thanks for letting me come with you. I guess that's the first fish I ever caught."

"Well, it won't be the last. We'll see to that. Don't be a stranger."

Chapter Nine

On Tuesday morning Lucas was back in his office in Dallas with a resolve he'd never experienced before. He would talk with Thomas Bennington, Sr. before the week was over or die trying. His first instinct was to call for an appointment, but he nixed that. Why would a man like Bennington agree to spend time with someone he didn't know—a young attorney from a new, relatively small law practice? He opted for his next idea. He'd show up in Bennington's office unannounced and stay until the man would see him. And he *would* play the lawyer card if it seemed to be the only way.

"I'll be out of the office for an extra-long lunch break, but you know where I'll be," he told Coop. "Call me if something comes up and I need to rush back. Otherwise, I'm just taking care of some personal business if anyone asks."

"Good luck."

"Thanks. I'm likely going to need a lot more than luck."

Lucas rode the elevator down to the parking garage and got in his gray Toyota. He took some deep breaths before starting the engine. It was out-of-character for him, but he switched on the radio to a classic country station. He guessed he still had a little of Trinity Springs in his system. Anyway, it helped calm his nerves as he sang along with Willie and Merle and Waylon.

His plan was to pop in on Thomas Bennington and show him the birth certificate. Lucas thought he could judge by the man's reaction whether he knew Everett Bennington. He had to lay it all out on the table. Didn't know any other way.

He parked on the street and walked a block to the glass building in downtown Dallas, took the escalator to the second floor, and entered the offices of Bennington and Bennington Enterprises. A bespectacled red-haired lady, in her fifties or sixties would be his guess, sat at the reception desk. "I'm Lucas Avila. Here to see Thomas Bennington, Sr.," he said with all the bravado he could muster.

"Do you have an appointment, Mr. Avila?"

"No, ma'am, but this is an important matter."

"Let me check with his executive assistant." She picked up the phone and punched in some numbers. "There's a Mr. Lucas Avila here and he wants to see Mr. Bennington."

Lucas supposed the assistant asked if he had an appointment, and the red-haired lady said, "He doesn't have an appointment, but he says it's important... Yes, I'll tell him." She put the receiver back in its cradle and looked up at Lucas. "Mr. Bennington sees people by appointment only."

He pulled out his business card and laid it in front of her. "I'm an attorney, and this is an urgent personal matter. Would you try again, please?"

She sighed, picked the phone back up, and dialed again. "Karen, Mr. Avila is an attorney and says it's an urgent personal matter... Okay. I'll hold... I'll tell him. You want him to wait here?" She put the phone down again. "Miss Blaine will be out in a minute. You can wait over there." She pointed to an ivory leather sofa across the room.

Lucas had barely gotten seated when he heard the *click click click* of high heels on the marble floor. The woman had on a navy suit and crisp white blouse. Her hair was blonde, short, and straight. She didn't seem much older than thirty-five or forty, but she was all business, this one. "Mr. Avila, I'm Karen Blaine, Mr. Bennington's assistant. Would you like to come into my office?"

Said the spider to the fly was the first thing that came to mind, but he rose and followed her. "Of course. Thank you for seeing me."

"Save your thanks for later. You might not need it." She motioned him into a large corner office with windows on two sides overlooking the Uptown area of Dallas. He wondered what her boss's office looked like if this was hers. "Have a seat. What can I do for you?"

"I came to see Mr. Bennington. It's a personal matter."

"All of Mr. Bennington's business goes through me first."

"Miss Blaine, with all due respect, this is not business as usual. As I said, it's a personal matter, and I don't think Mr. Bennington would be happy if I discussed it with anyone other than him."

"Lila said you're an attorney?"

"Yes, ma'am. I am."

"What firm?"

"I'm with Benson and Hughes, but this doesn't concern my employer."

"I see. What *does* it concern?"

"Miss Blaine, I know you're just doing your job, but what I have to discuss with Thomas Bennington is a personal, family matter. Now I can see him here, or I can show up at his house. If I do that, I'll tell him I tried to see him at his office first. I don't think he'll be pleased if I take this matter to his home when he's with his family. It will be much better for your boss if I see him here in his office." There. He'd laid it all out. Sink or swim.

"You're persistent. I'll give you that."

"Yes, ma'am."

"Don't call me ma'am. It makes me feel old."

"No, ma'am. I mean... I'm sorry. It's how I was raised, and it's a hard habit to break."

"I can't imagine what this could possibly be about, but I'm going to break one of my rules and contact Mr. Bennington. I'll ask him if he wants to see you. Then it will be up to him, not me."

"I appreciate that."

"Stay here. I'm going to his office. I'll be back shortly to let you know his answer."

"Thank you, ma'—Miss Blaine."

When the executive assistant left, Lucas took his birth certificate out of his pocket and examined it again. He didn't know why. Maybe he was trying to reassure himself that the name he'd seen really was Bennington. But as many times as he'd looked at it, the name hadn't changed. His father, at least according to his birth certificate, was Everett Bennington. And Cooper had found out from his mother that Thomas Bennington had a second son who'd disappeared several years ago. Every time he added two and two it came out four...and the thought unnerved him.

He tried for more deep breaths, but only short, shallow ones came this time. The longer Miss Blaine was gone, the more nervous he became. *Please hurry before I lose my nerve completely. I've come too far to quit now.*

In what seemed like an eternity to Lucas but in reality was only a couple more minutes, the door opened and she said, "Mr. Bennington will see you. Follow me."

He rose and wiped his sweaty palms on the sides of his suit pants. The woman took him down a short hall to another corner office even larger and with more windows overlooking Dallas than the one he'd been in previously.

Stay strong, Lucas. Then wise words of Papa Joe came to him. *He puts his pants on one leg at a time just like you do.*

"Thank you, Miss Blaine. Please close the door on your way out," said the man with white hair and the palest blue eyes Lucas had ever seen. "Have a seat, young man."

"Thank you, sir."

"What can I do for you?"

"My name is Lucas Avila. I was raised by my grandparents in Trinity Springs, about an hour north of Dallas."

"I know where it is. Get to the point, Mr. Avila."

"My grandparents are both deceased now, and I was cleaning out the house and came across a document I'd like you to look at. It's my birth certificate, and there's a name on there that I'd never heard before. I haven't seen my mother since I was three, and my grandparents never mentioned my father."

"What does this have to do with me? You have this document with you?"

"Yes, sir." Lucas reached in his inside coat pocket, pulled it out, unfolded it, and laid it on Thomas Bennington's desk. "Do you know an Everett Bennington? Could he possibly be a relative of yours?"

The color drained from the man's face as he stared at the birth certificate. "I don't know a person by that name. Must be another set of Benningtons." He pushed the paper back toward Lucas.

"Are you sure? Could it be a cousin, nephew, or distant relative maybe?"

"This has nothing to do with me. I'm not even sure that document isn't forged. What did you hope to gain by coming here, young man?"

"Certainly nothing in the way of financial gain, sir. I'm an attorney and am happy with my station in life. My maternal grandparents gave me a wonderful upbringing and education, but they're both gone now. I was just hoping to connect with my biological father, if he's willing.

I haven't wanted to search for my mother since she abandoned me, but if I have to find her to locate my father, I will. I'm sure I could find her quite easily through an aunt."

"When and where did you say you discovered the document?"

"About a week ago at my grandparents' house when I was cleaning it out to sell."

"That was the first time you'd seen it?"

"Yes, sir."

"Well, Lucas... May I call you Lucas?"

"Of course."

"I'm going to ask you not to mention this to anyone else. If you will promise to do that, I might be able to help you."

"Yes, sir. I appreciate it."

"Would you be willing to take a DNA test?"

There it was. Mr. Bennington was finally acknowledging the possibility that they could be related. Breathing a sigh of relief, Lucas said, "Yes, I would. I suppose that would answer a lot of questions."

"This is between you and me, you understand. I'm not making any promises."

"I understand. Thank you, sir. I appreciate your meeting with me. Would you like me to arrange to take the test?"

"If you'll give me your number, I'll be in touch about that test. It will be done privately, and I'll make the arrangements and cover the expense."

Lucas put a business card on Thomas's desk and picked up his birth certificate. "The second number is my cell. Call me any time, sir. And thank you again for seeing me."

"I'll have Miss Blaine walk you out." He picked up his phone and touched one button. "Miss Blaine, Mr. Avila is ready to leave. Will you walk him out, please, and then come back to my office?"

She accompanied him all the way down the escalator and to the outside door. *Is she afraid I won't leave the building or something?* And he laughed to himself about the ridiculousness of the whole situation. *A grown man who has to have a young woman take care of business for him. I hope I never get that rich and helpless.*

Lucas grabbed a burger from a food truck across the street and walked the block back to his car. Since he'd used up his entire lunch hour and then some, he ate with one hand and drove with the other, hoping he wouldn't have a lap full of mustard when he got back to the office.

"Karen, if that young man ever calls or comes back to the office, put him straight through to me without question. And tell Lila to do the same," Thomas said when his assistant was back in his office.

"Yes, sir, but—"

"No buts. He doesn't need to talk to anyone except me. Is that clear?"

"It is."

"Thank you. That'll be all for now." He looked down, picked up his pen, and started writing.

Chapter Ten

Wednesday came and went, leaving Lucas wondering when he was supposed to take the revealing DNA test. But on Thursday morning at ten o'clock sharp his phone rang, and an unfamiliar number appeared on the screen. "Lucas Avila speaking."

"Lucas, it's Thomas Bennington."

"Yes, sir." His heart began to race.

"Shortly you will receive a call from William Browning of Alda Laboratories. He'll set up the time and place for the DNA test. This is my personal number I'm calling on. Make a note of it, and if you need to reach me for anything, call this number. You don't need to go through my assistant or receptionist."

"I understand. Thank you for making the arrangements."

"I'm having the results rushed, and I'll speak with you after they come in."

Lucas sat motionless, staring at the picture on the wall opposite his desk. The situation was getting real. Soon he would know. He'd either be the grandson of one of the wealthiest and most influential men in Dallas, or he'd be back at square one, having no idea who or where Everett Bennington was. Then it hit him. *I wonder if Thomas Bennington has enough money and influence to pay off a lab and convince them to lie about DNA results.* He resolved, at that moment, if he suspected that might have happened, he would find his mother and take a different route to solve the issue of who his father was.

His phone rang again, and it startled him. Another number he didn't recognize. He took a deep breath. "Lucas Avila speaking."

"Mr. Avila, this is William Browning from Alda Laboratories. I'm calling for Mr. Thomas Bennington. He wants me to do a DNA analysis on you as soon as possible. Could you come to my office today?"

They're not wasting any time. I hope that's a good sign. "I'm at work right now. How late are you open?"

"Do you get a lunch break? Your part won't take long." *When he said 'as soon as possible,' he meant it.*

"I do," Lucas said. "Where is your office located?"

Lucas took down the address and suite number and arranged to meet there at twelve-thirty. Then he leaned back in his chair, put his head against the headrest, and closed his eyes. *What are you doing, Lucas? What do you hope to gain?* It was a question Mr. Bennington had asked him, and now he was confronted with it again. He had no interest at all in getting to know Thomas Bennington and the family, from what he'd learned of them. And if Everett Bennington was their son, they probably didn't know where he was anyway. What was to be gained by pursuing this?

But he was too far into it now to back out. He would take the DNA test and wait for the results.

"We can do this with a cheek swab, Mr. Avila," William Browning said as soon as Lucas entered the private office suite. "I'll send the results to Mr. Bennington, probably tomorrow, and I assume he will get in touch with you after that. We're putting a rush on it. I want you to be assured that I'm doing this in the strictest confidence."

"I appreciate your help, Mr. Browning."

Lucas showed his picture ID and signed a consent form. The swab took about two seconds, and he was glad he'd have time today to eat a normal lunch. Yesterday's burger had given him indigestion because he'd wolfed it down so fast. Or maybe because he'd been a bundle of nerves after his visit to Bennington's office.

"That's all I need from you," the man said. "I don't know what this is about, but I wish you the best."

"Thank you for getting to it so fast."

"Well, as you might or might not know, Mr. Bennington can be quite persuasive."

"Yes, sir. I imagine that's true," Lucas replied as he exited the office.

He took his cell out of his pocket and punched in Cooper's number. "Hey. Are you still at the office?"

"Yeah. Finishing up some paperwork on the Taylor case."

"I got finished with my errand sooner than I expected. Want to meet at Sol's for a quick bite? I'll get there before you, and I can order for both of us."

"Sure. I'll be there as soon as I can."

Cooper entered the restaurant as the server was putting a large platter of barbecued ribs and sides of baked beans and potato salad on the table. "Smells great! What's going on? You were so secretive when you left the office."

"And I have to be for a while longer, but I might be able to tell you more tomorrow. I'm sure you know generally what it's about."

"Well, I have an idea."

"And your idea would be right, but I'm sworn to secrecy until we know more."

"Okay. You didn't tell me anything, but I can draw a conclusion. I'm sure you're on pins and needles waiting to know more."

"No kidding! I wasn't this nervous waiting to hear if I'd passed the bar exam."

The night was cool and the sky was clear in Trinity Springs. Maria couldn't imagine being anywhere other than on her patio with her guitar in hand. What did people have against fresh air? Why did so many of them stay closed up in their houses when they could enjoy the outdoors on a beautiful night like this?

Lucas had been back in Dallas for a couple of days, but he would be in Trinity Springs again on Friday afternoon, and she was looking forward to seeing him then. This time she had a proposition for him. Sherise's sixty-fifth birthday was coming up in about a month, and Maria wanted to plan a surprise party for her. Surely Lucas would want in on the preparations. Sherise had played such a big role in his life. Planning it together would be fun, and she already had some ideas.

As she strummed her guitar, Maria ran through some of those ideas in her mind. They would need a place large enough to hold a crowd because Sherise knew almost everyone in town. They would need donations if they were going to serve food, but she knew plenty of people who would probably pitch in. And last, they would need entertainment. Sherise loved music, especially Motown and country. That might be a little more difficult. Maria could perform a few songs, but she wanted something special...something Sherise didn't hear often. She'd have to think on that, and maybe Lucas would have some ideas or connections.

She'd text him tomorrow, but tonight seemed to call for all four verses of "How Great Thou Art." She especially liked the second and third verses, which most people usually skipped over. As she began to play and sing, a peace fell over her as it so often did when she sang her favorite hymn.

On Friday morning Lucas had his nose buried in paperwork for a case he was preparing for court when his cell vibrated on his desk, and it startled him.

"Lucas, Thomas Bennington here. The DNA analysis results were just delivered to my office. Can you come in today?"

As he held the phone to his ear, he noticed his hand was shaking slightly and his breathing was more labored than usual. This was the call he'd been waiting for, but he didn't expect it so soon. "Yes, sir. My lunch break is in an hour."

"Fine. Fine. My assistant is out today, but I've instructed the receptionist to let you through. Do you remember how to get to my office from the reception area?"

"Yes, sir, I do."

"I'll see you a little after noon then."

"I'll be there. Thank you for letting me know." He laid the phone back down on his desk, but try as he might, he couldn't get his mind back on work. Too much was at stake.

Lucas grabbed his keys at twelve o'clock and left his office, not telling Cooper where he was going. He didn't want to waste any time. His foot rested a little heavier than usual on the pedal when he hit the tollway, but he was chomping at the bit to find out the results of the test.

He parked his car about two blocks away from Bennington and Bennington Enterprises this time and power-walked to the building. He took the escalator but walked up it as fast as he could, barely said hello to the red-haired receptionist, and started down the hall to Thomas Bennington's office. The door was open, but he still hesitated and knocked on the doorframe.

"Come in and have a seat." Mr. Bennington rose, walked around his desk, seated himself in the chair beside Lucas, and turned toward him. "It seems highly likely that you are my grandson."

"How likely, sir?" he asked, his heart pounding.

"Ninety-nine point nine percent."

Lucas sat up a little straighter in his chair. "Wow. That's definitive, isn't it?"

"Here's the deal," Thomas continued without hesitation. "I have no idea where your biological father is, but I'm going to give you $50,000 now and every year from here on out. I'm also changing my will to reflect that the payment will continue after my death. In response to this, I expect you to say nothing to anyone about this revelation. In fact, I've had my attorney draw up a nondisclosure agreement for you to sign. If you vary from this agreement, the money will be cut off. Do you understand the terms?"

Lucas blinked a few times, processing, letting the request sink in. "I understand the terms, sir, but I don't want the money. I want to meet my father. And to know the story of how he and my mother met. If you don't know where he is, I have other ways of trying to find out. Thank you for the generous offer, but I can't sign the NDA because that would preclude me from trying to locate Everett Bennington. Don't you want to know where he is?"

"You don't understand the situation," Thomas said. "It's complex."

"I'm sure it is, but I hope you understand that I have to try. My grandparents who raised me are gone now, and there's an empty spot in my life I believe he might be able to fill. I guess you could say I'm looking for my roots and I need to feel grounded. Fifty thousand dollars a year wouldn't do that for me. I'm sorry."

"Can't be bought off. Unusual in someone your age. I admire that. Can I at least ask you to be discreet in your search? Unfortunately, I have a high profile family in this city, and I need to look out for the interests of my wife and my other son and his family too."

"I understand your concern, and I will be very discreet. Would you like me to keep you posted if I discover something I think you might want to know?"

"You have my personal number. You can call me directly anytime."

"Do you have any information at all? I know you said you don't know where he is, but if I could have just a little something to go on, that might help with my search. Where he lived? What he was doing twenty-seven years ago?"

"I've given you all I'm going to be able to give you with the DNA results."

"And I do appreciate that," Lucas said. "You don't know how my mother and father met?"

"I do not. I'm sorry to cut this short, but I have a meeting at one."

As Lucas reached out to shake the man's hand, it occurred to him that he was shaking the hand of his paternal grandfather, who just happened to be one of the richest men in Dallas. It sent a tingle through his arm and into his spine and was the last thing he would have expected when he opened that drawer in his grandmother's bedroom.

Chapter Eleven

Thomas Bennington felt the knot in his stomach tighten as he thought about the lie he'd told Lucas Avila a couple of hours earlier. It wasn't as though he hadn't been untruthful many times in the course of building a multi-million dollar business. No, he was quite used to a bit of fabricating here and there. But this time the act had been a punch in the gut for him, and he couldn't figure out why it continued to eat at him even after his meeting with the board of directors.

Was it because the young man had impressed him with his manners and his refusal to take a very generous bribe? Who in his right mind would reject an offer of $50,000 a year without even thinking about it? He wasn't used to such virtue in the business world. Which made his deceit that much more distasteful to him.

But what could be done about it? He couldn't tell him the truth now. That was a hornet's nest he wasn't about to stir. The effect could be devastating to him and his family.

Neither Sally nor Thomas, Jr. knew this secret, and he had no intention of changing that now.

Having a private detective on retainer had come in handy as he'd built his business from the ground up. Max McBride was able to dig up dirt on just about anyone in the corporate world. He got Max on the phone. "Max. Thomas Bennington here."

"Haven't heard from you in a while, Mr. B. I was feeling kind of guilty taking your money every month with nothing to do. Just kidding! I'm actually fine with that." He laughed. "What can I do for you? I hope it's something good. I'm a little bored right now."

"Has there been any change in his location?"

"Just from his winter digs to his summer place. Made the transition about a week ago."

"Okay. Keep a closer eye on him than usual and let me know if anything changes."

"Is that all ya got? I was hoping for something a little more stimulating."

"There is one more thing."

"Spill it."

"See what you can find on a young man named Lucas Avila. He's with Benson and Hughes law firm."

"Now that's more like it. Something I can sink my teeth into. What info do you have? Address? Phone number? Birthdate? Physical description?"

Thomas remembered Lucas's birthdate from his quick glance at the birth certificate and gave that piece of information to Max, along with his phone number and color of hair and eyes. "That's all I have, Max. I'm sure you can use that to get started."

"Sure. No problem. I'll see what I can find. Call you soon."

"Call me directly on this line. Don't go through Karen on this one."

"Sure 'nuff, boss. How *is* that drill sergeant of yours?"

"She does what I need her to do. But this is personal, and she knows nothing about it. I trust you to be discreet as you always have been."

"That's what you pay me for, and I still like those thick, juicy steaks your money buys me. I'll holler back at you soon."

Thomas rolled his chair back and put his head on his desk. Although he was seventy-five years old, retiring had never before been an option for him. But now he was beginning to feel as though it might be getting close to time. The business was beginning to take its toll on his health, and the directors weren't making it any easier. So much had changed since he'd started the company over forty years ago, and he was thinking it might be time for Thomas, Jr. to take the reins.

Sally wouldn't be happy to have him underfoot, but he could probably find some pastime to get out of the house. He'd never taken up golf, but maybe it wasn't too late to start. Or he could buy a sailboat. That might be easier. At least there wouldn't be a huge learning curve, and they lived close to White Rock Lake. And when the weather wasn't good for sailing, he could always sit in his study and read.

Yes, retirement might be just what he needed.

On Friday afternoon the city faded into the distance behind Lucas as he made his way north to Trinity Springs. This time he wasn't dreading going back, and he wondered if it had something to do with a certain young woman he'd recently reconnected with. He knew he had a lot to do but hoped to spend some time with her as well. Thoughts of Maria kept him from obsessing over Thomas and Everett Bennington and the results of the DNA test. So much had happened in ten days.

He pulled up in his driveway, but instead of going into the house, he crossed the street and knocked on Maria's door, hoping she would be home from school by six o'clock. Surely she didn't work this late on a Friday.

"Lucas. Hi. I didn't expect to see you today."

Lucas was taken aback again at the sight of her. This time she wore workout clothes with her dark brown hair pulled back in a ponytail, and his heart was doing little flip-flops in his chest. "I should have called or texted first. I'm sorry. Is this an inconvenient time?"

"No. I didn't mean that. I just didn't know you'd be back in Trinity Springs this early."

"Thought I'd better get a jumpstart on cleaning out…but…I'm hungry, so I was wondering if you'd like to grab a bite to eat first. That is, if you haven't already eaten."

"I haven't. So…yeah. Where do you want to go?"

"Sherise's?"

"Could we go someplace different? I have something to talk over with you, and it's not something that Sherise should overhear." She smiled and her eyes lit up mischievously. "Have I piqued your curiosity?"

"Yes, you have. Where would you like to go? I'm fine with anything."

"What about Uncle Rio's Barbecue?"

"Sure. I'll drive this time."

Maria grabbed her purse and they crossed the street to Lucas's car. As he opened the passenger door for her, he wondered if this would count as a date. An informal and impromptu one…but maybe.

When Lucas pulled his Toyota sedan into the parking lot at the restaurant, the car was surrounded on all sides by a gaggle of pickup trucks. More trucks together in one place than he had seen in a long time. Inside, Uncle Rio's was hopping with people, and it was loud. Very loud. Lucas couldn't remember a time when the place was this crowded. Maria waved at a couple of her students who were there with their parents.

They made their way through the buffet line and found a booth in the back of the restaurant where he hoped they could hear each other.

"It seems we're not the only people who wanted barbecue tonight. I wonder if Sherise has any customers," he said.

"I imagine she does. Trinity Springs likes to go out to eat on Friday night."

"I'm really curious about what you didn't want her to hear." He put their plates and drinks on the table and handed the trays to a busboy before sitting down.

"You know her birthday's coming up in about a month," Maria said as soon as he was seated across from her.

"That's right." Sherise's birthday had always been a big deal to her, and for the entire month of April each meal at the café came with a free dessert.

"I was thinking about throwing her a surprise birthday party and wondered if you would want to help plan it. I'm sure my friend Kacie and my parents will help. But I thought you might enjoy having a hand in it."

"Well…" While Lucas wanted to jump at the chance to spend more time with Maria, he was feeling a little stressed with everything that was going on in his life. Preparing the case at work. Cleaning out the house. Searching for his father. Planning a party for Sherise would be fun, but could he—should he—take on another task?

"Don't feel obligated. I just thought…" Maria's voice trailed off.

"No, it's not that I wouldn't want to. But I have a lot going on right now…at work…and personally."

"I see."

Lucas hated to hear what sounded like disappointment in her voice. "What kind of time involvement would it take?"

"As much or as little as you have to give. I understand. I know you're only here on weekends and when you are, you need to be working on the house. I get it. I probably shouldn't have mentioned it."

"I'd really like to help if I can. How far are you in the planning?"

"Square one." Maria sighed, dabbed at barbecue sauce in the corner of her mouth, and brushed away an unruly strand of dark brown hair that was determined to cover her left eye. "I just had the idea a couple of days ago and haven't mentioned it to anyone else. But you know Trinity Springs and Sherise. Everyone loves her. I hope we can keep it a secret."

"Do you have a venue in mind?" *I wish you'd leave your hair alone. It looks sexy falling over your eye like that.*

"I'm going to talk to Paul about using the fellowship hall at church. It's pretty big, with plenty of tables and chairs. It even has a platform so we could have some entertainment. You know how she loves music."

"Are you the entertainment?" Lucas asked. "I just realized I've never heard you sing."

"She's heard me plenty of times. I was thinking about getting some of my students to work up a little show for her. Some country. Some Motown. Some classics."

"I'm sure she would love that. What can I do to help?"

"Maybe help getting the word out. Not sure how to do that yet."

"Sure. I can do that. I'm thinking about buying Isabel's third of the house. That way she won't have to worry about it, and I won't have to rush to get it cleaned out. Plus…I'll have to locate my mother. According to the will, she owns the other third." He longed to tell Maria the other reason he needed to locate his mother—to find his father—and the real reason he didn't want to sell the house. He wouldn't have a place to stay when he came back to visit, and he was hoping to have a reason to come back often.

"Have you tried to find her? Your mother?"

"Never wanted to. I always felt hurt that she abandoned me…but now I think it was probably for the best. It would have been hard for an uneducated single mom to raise a kid. And she knew Papa Joe and Mama Rosa would give me a stable home and plenty of love."

"So you can't sell the house until you find her, can you?"

"That's right."

"I wish I could say I'm sorry about that, but I'm not." Maria smiled and Lucas's heart skipped a beat.

Chapter Twelve

Max McBride donned a baseball cap and sunglasses and drove to downtown Dallas, not sure where he would find Everett Bennington but certain that he could. He'd located Thomas's son fifteen years ago and had been keeping an eye on him since. He knew most, if not all, of Everett's hangouts. He'd try the library first. That was Everett's favorite summer spot, and Max knew exactly which floor to check first.

He whipped his red BMW into one of the few open spaces in the parking garage below the library and took the elevator to the eighth floor. He recognized the cute blonde girl behind the circulation desk and had seen her interact with Everett. *If I were only ten years younger,* Max thought...*okay, twenty.* He surreptitiously searched the entire floor with no luck, so he took the elevator down to the sixth, where the political science books were housed. A quick look around the floor didn't produce Everett either, so he decided to drive to Cadiz Street. Maybe he'd see him walking. Maybe he'd find him standing guard over his friends' belongings. Max knew they took turns, and Everett, or Benny as his friends on the street called him, did more than his share of playing watchdog.

He wasn't there either, but Max recognized the man on duty. He'd heard Everett refer to him as Shane. If only he could go up to Shane and say, "Hey, where's your buddy Benny today?" But he'd been playing it by the book for fifteen years, and he couldn't change his tactics now. The boss expected him to remain an unknown entity to his wayward son and paid him well for maintaining secrecy.

There was one other place he could check. A gas station owner a few blocks to the east had been known to allow Everett and a few other select homeless veterans to use his restroom to freshen up. They'd gained his trust several years ago, and as far as Max knew, this station was the only place they had to shower during the summer. The owner Isaiah, also a veteran, had added a shower in the large restroom several years ago for just that purpose, knowing that without the help of a supportive family he might be in the same situation.

But before he reached the station, Max spotted Everett, cleanly shaven and with what appeared to be a recent haircut. He had on clean clothes and carried his duffel. He'd already taken his shower and was headed back to either his spot on the street or the library. Max had seen all he needed to see, though. Thomas's son was clean and appeared to be healthy. Mr. Bennington would be pleased to get the report.

Max's next stop was the records building. He'd started his search for information on Lucas Avila but hadn't completed it, and the boss wanted to hear as soon as possible.

Two hours later, Thomas Bennington picked up his phone on the first ring. "What do you have for me, Max?"

"He was clean, had his summer haircut, and his winter beard was gone. He's ready for warmer weather and apparently still able to use Isaiah's restroom to freshen up."

"That's good. That's good." Thomas nodded his head as if Max could see him. "Had he lost weight?"

"Didn't appear to have lost any. He looked fit as a fiddle."

"I guess he's getting enough to eat then."

"That appears to be the case."

"What about the other task I gave you?"

"That boy's squeaky clean. Made one B in high school…in calculus…but who didn't, huh? Only a few in college and ranked in the top ten percent of his law class. Never sent to the principal's office. No problems on any social media sites. Isn't married. No arrests…not even a speeding ticket. What are you doing keeping company with such a boring guy, Mr. B?"

"Max, I'm going to tell you something and I'm going to emphasize that you treat this information with the same confidentiality you've always afforded me, keeping in mind what I pay you to be discreet."

"Absolutely. You can count on me, boss."

Thomas originally had no intention of telling anyone, but he blurted it out. "That boy is Everett's son."

After a few seconds, Max cleared his throat and spoke. "Well…knock me over with a feather. I didn't think to check his birth certificate. How did you find out?"

"I don't have time to go into it right now, but I'll fill you in soon. I'll just tell you this much. I tried to buy him off with fifty thousand a year and an NDA, and he'd have none of it. Dead set on finding his father."

"You don't say."

"I told a little white lie, Max."

"*No*! Mr. B, you *didn't*."

"I'm not paying you to be impertinent…but I guess you know me too well."

"I'll admit most of your—shall we say—*untruths* are a bit more colorful than white. You told him you didn't know where Everett was, didn't you?"

"I did. Can you imagine what this would do to Sally and Thomas, Jr. if it hit the papers? No...as long as Everett's doing okay, I'm not going to rock the boat. And I'm going to see that no one else rocks it either. Get back to me if you find out anything I need to know."

"You got it, boss."

Thomas had no problem keeping the secret of his knowing Everett's whereabouts from his wife. Sally never mentioned Everett. They hadn't talked about him in years. He supposed it was too painful for a mother to continue to grieve a child she'd essentially lost, so she'd put her second son out of her mind. Everyone in the family knew not to bring him up around her too.

In all fairness, Thomas had to admit that he also grieved the loss. Even though he knew Everett's situation, he couldn't just go up to him and say, "Hi, son. How about coming home?" Their son had made it painfully clear when he left home that he no longer wanted to be a part of the family.

Sally had been the one to find the note, but Thomas kept it in his desk drawer at work. He took it out, removed it from its ivory envelope, and read it for probably the one-hundredth time.

I'm leaving. Don't try to find me. I'm not cut out to be in this family. I don't want the same things you want. Leave me alone and let me find my own way. I hope you understand.   Everett

He folded the note, slipped it into the envelope, and put it back in the drawer under some ledgers. Max McBride was the only person besides Sally and Thomas, Jr. who knew about it. Even Karen wasn't privy to this part of his life. Max had proved himself to be trustworthy in personal dealings over the years. He wasn't so sure about his executive assistant.

Chapter Thirteen

Lucas woke up Saturday morning dreading what he knew had to be done. He would have to talk to his aunt. Maybe Isabel knew where her sister was. It was a long shot, but he had to take it. He also wanted to see how she felt about having the house appraised and selling her third. He thought she'd be happy to get the money and not have to worry about it any longer, but he'd never been able to read her. Isabel was an enigma. Always had been. Moody as a teenager and even moodier after she left home.

He reluctantly dialed her cell. She answered on the second ring. "Hello, Lucas. Do you have the house cleaned out? Have you talked to a realtor?"

"Not yet, Isabel, but I need to talk to you. In person. Do you want to come over here, or should I come to your place?"

"When will you have it ready to sell?" Lucas could tell she wasn't in the mood to chitchat.

"That's what I need to talk to you about."

"Can't you tell me over the phone?" She obviously wasn't in the mood to see him either.

"I'd rather not."

"Oh, all right," Isabel conceded. "I can be there in thirty minutes."

"Have you had breakfast? I could make omelets…or scrambled eggs."

"I don't want any breakfast. I'll take some coffee, though."

"Sure. I'll see you then." Lucas set his phone beside him on the bed and stared out the window at the blue house across the street. Compared to Isabel, Maria was so much easier to talk with. Well, if he were being honest, he'd have to admit that she was easy to talk with compared to just about anyone he'd ever known.

He finished getting dressed and went to the kitchen to put on a fresh pot of coffee. Why was he dreading this meeting with Isabel so much? Maybe because there was a lot riding on it. Maybe because he'd never known how to get through to her. She could refuse to sell him her portion of the house and insist they put it on the market immediately. The sale was contingent on their finding Carmen, though, so if Isabel knew where his mother was, she'd have to tell him. He was executor of the will. He'd have to be the one to tell Carmen about Mama Rosa's death…if she didn't already know.

As soon as he'd cleared off the table, unloaded the dishwasher, and gotten two mugs out of the cabinet, he heard a knock at the door and went to answer it.

"Good morning. There's coffee in the kitchen. It's good to see you again."

No hello. No hug. Isabel walked past him and headed for the kitchen. "I can't imagine why we couldn't have this discussion over the phone," she called over her shoulder.

Lucas followed her into the kitchen and poured two mugs of steaming coffee, setting one on the table in front of her. "It might be a little more complicated than you think it's going to be."

"What's complicated about cleaning out the house and calling a realtor? Then we split the money."

"You know Mama Rosa had a will, right?"

"I hadn't thought about it. So?"

"So. If she had died without a will, fifty percent of the estate would have gone to you, and fifty percent would have gone to Carmen. I would get nothing since they didn't officially adopt me."

"But you say she did have one. So?"

"The will states that you, Carmen, and I each get a third of the estate."

"What does Carmen have to do with any of this anyway?"

"Half of the estate without a will. One third *with* the will, which has to be probated. Of course, we have to find her first. Which is why I wanted to talk to you."

"What do I have to do with Carmen? She left years ago...as you well know."

"Maybe nothing. Maybe you *don't* know where she is. But I've heard that you two were close growing up. I thought maybe..."

Isabel looked down and picked at the red and white plaid tablecloth. "I don't know anything."

"Look at me, Isabel, and tell me that." Lucas knew enough about jury selection and witness questioning to recognize the signs when someone was lying, and he had a strong feeling Isabel knew more than she was willing to admit. Her failure to make eye contact spoke volumes.

His aunt continued to run her finger over the tablecloth and said nothing.

"Isabel. That's my mother...your sister. Papa and Mama are gone, and she's our only other living close relative. If you know something, I deserve to know it too. You don't get to make the rules...and she doesn't get to make the rules. I have a stake in this, and I'm not talking about just the sale of the house. For years I didn't care. I had everything—and everyone—I needed right here. She abandoned me, so I didn't want to know her. But things are different now. I need to locate her for a reason other than just the house sale."

"What other reason?"

"I need her to help me find my father."

"Your *father*?" Isabel finally looked up and locked eyes with her nephew.

"Yes."

"What makes you think she would do that?"

"I have a name."

"You do not."

"I do."

"How?"

"I found my birth certificate."

"Where?"

"That's not important. What's important is that I find my biological parents. You always knew yours. I deserve to know mine, don't you think?"

"That's not what Carmen wanted."

"No? Well, consider these two things. One, why did she list my father's name on my birth certificate if she didn't want me to ever know? And two, why did Mama Rosa include her in the will knowing we would have to find her to probate and divide up the estate?"

Isabel got up from the table and headed for the kitchen door. She turned and looked back at Lucas. "Call me when you're ready to sell the house. Otherwise, I'd just as soon not know what you're doing."

"I want to buy your third."

The scowl on her face told him she wasn't amenable to the idea. "What?"

"I want to buy your third of the house."

"Why?"

"You want out from under it, don't you? You don't want to have to worry about the upkeep. You apparently want the money as soon as possible. So I'm willing to pay you for your third of the house now. We can have it appraised. And when the estate is probated, you'll get your third of that too. The sale of the furniture and what little is left in the checking account."

"What's in it for you?" Isabel's dark brown eyes flashed with irritation.

"Not that I owe you an explanation, but I'm thinking about keeping the house."

"For heaven's sake, *why*? Why would you want a house in Trinity Springs when you live and work in Dallas? That doesn't make sense, Lucas."

"To tell you the truth, I've enjoyed spending some time in Trinity Springs again. I'll use it as a weekend getaway. Sometimes it's good to get out of the city. Enjoy the quiet of a small town. Be able to go to the lake for a little fishing maybe."

"Since when do you fish?"

"Since I visited the Vargases at Cypress Grove last weekend."

Isabel gave Lucas a knowing look. "You're keen on Maria, aren't you?"

"And if I were? Would that be a problem for you?"

"No. I don't really care one way or the other what you do."

"Then you won't mind if I decide to keep the house."

"Like I said… I don't care. Draw up the papers. I'll sell you my part of the house. I'll be glad to get rid of it. You can call the plumber when the sink backs up. You can mow the yard when the weeds get too high. You can spray for bugs in the summertime. All of that joy will be yours now. Let me know when and where to sign and give me a check."

"Thank you, Isabel."

"But don't try to find Carmen. She doesn't want to be found." Isabel opened the front door.

"Wait!" Lucas stepped in front of her and closed the door. "What do you mean? How do you know?"

"Just take my word for it. Let me go, Lucas. Call me when you have my check ready." He moved out of her way and she stomped out, slamming the door behind her.

As Lucas replayed their conversation in his mind, he couldn't help thinking Isabel knew more than she was willing to tell him. He suspected his aunt might have either heard from Carmen or heard from someone else who knew where she was and what she was doing. But he understood Isabel well enough to realize she would never open up to him, so he'd have to think of another way to find his mother.

It kind of amazed him that he'd lived his whole life up to now neither knowing nor caring where his biological parents were. He had everything he needed right here in Trinity Springs—right here in this house. But now. Now something was different. The death of Mama Rosa had left a vacuum in his life. A hollow place that needed to be filled. And he felt the only way to fill that gap was to discover his roots.

Chapter Fourteen

Lucas finished packing his grandmother's clothes and shoes into boxes to take to Goodwill and moved into the garage to tackle his grandfather's tools. As he worked, he continued to hear Isabel's sharp voice telling him his mother didn't want to be found. *She knows something. It's pretty obvious.*

He'd already checked the social media sites, but Carmen Avila was a common name and he had no idea what she looked like now or where she lived…or even whether she was married and had a different last name. He felt as though he was up against a brick wall. Could he find some way to persuade his aunt to tell him what she knew?

He'd promised Sherise to come back more often, so he worked in the garage until noon and decided to pay her another visit. He needed some of her sage advice and was craving her chicken potpie.

It had been many years since Lucas had walked to downtown Trinity Springs, but it was a glorious spring day and he couldn't resist. Something about being back home soothed his soul and cleared his mind. Weekends had become mini-vacations. A retreat from the concrete and bustle of the city.

Birdsong and spring flowers along the way reassured him that his decision to ditch the car had been a wise one. How long had it been since he'd felt this peaceful? In the midst of so much uncertainty in his life, being here, breathing in fresh air unadulterated by highway traffic, proved to be just the balm he needed. Hearing happy shrieks of children playing in front yards and seeing them ride by on bikes transported him back to his own childhood and memories of a special little girl who had grown up to be someone who kept invading his thoughts. Someone with whom he wanted to spend more time. Wanted to get to know better.

He made it to the town square in just under twenty minutes. He used to make it in ten when he was a teenager and Mama Rosa would let him ride his bike. That old brown bike was still in the garage. Maybe he should air up the tires. Maybe even take it out to Mike's Bike Shop and treat it to a new paint job. Blue? Red? *I wonder if Maria has a bicycle and likes to ride.* Why did every thought seem to circle back to Maria? He needed to get a grip.

He spotted Sherise through the window as he approached the café. She was bent over a table looking at someone's phone…probably pictures of the couple's grandchildren. His mentor was interested in every aspect of her customers' lives. He used to think he was special, but as he'd grown older and wiser, he realized Sherise Washington was an equal opportunity friend and hugger. Actually, he suspected most of the people who knew Sherise thought they were her favorites. It was her superpower.

She spotted him as soon as he crossed the threshold. "Hey, you! I thought I might see you today. Can't stay away from Trinity Springs now, can you? I wonder why. Must be old Sherise. I'm such a magnet for young, good-looking, big-city attorneys."

He planted a kiss on her forehead. "It's always been you, Sherise."

"Maybe it used to be, but I know better now," she quipped with a wink.

"Hey," he said, trying to change the subject, "can a guy get a decent meal around here? And do you have time to talk?"

"Looks like your table's occupied. Come into my office. I'll tell Tina to take your order there. Give me just a minute to wrap up some unfinished business in the kitchen."

Lucas could never figure out how Sherise could find anything on her desk, but she was always able to put her finger immediately on anything she needed. He was afraid to move any papers, but when Tina came in to take his order, she cleaned off a corner, making just enough space for a plate.

"Sherise said you were gonna eat in here…just like old times, huh? I hope you're planning to make a habit of this. We've been missing you around here since Rosa passed."

"I think I will, Tina. I'm thinking about keeping the house so I'll have a place to stay when I come back on weekends."

"Comin' back on weekends now, are you? Hmmm… I wonder if it could have anything to do with a—"

"Don't you start. Sherise already teased me."

"Well, I know what I know." Tina ruffled Lucas's hair on top as she'd done most of his life.

"So I assume you know what I want for lunch today."

"I know what I know about matters of the heart, not the stomach."

"Chicken potpie for now and chicken fried steak to go. Surprise me again with the veggies. You hit the nail on the head last time. And sweet tea whenever you get a chance. No rush. I know you're busy."

"You got it." She scribbled something on her small notepad and stuck the pencil through the bun on the back of her head.

Sherise entered her office less than a minute after Tina had left to take Lucas's order to the kitchen. "Looks like either you or Tina made you some room to eat on the desk."

"Tina. You know I've always been scared to touch your papers. I might move something a sixteenth of an inch and you couldn't find it."

Sherise laughed. "You said you wanted to talk. I assume it's either about that lovely neighbor of yours, or—and this would be my bet—you've learned something about your father."

"How do you always know?" Lucas turned his palms up and shrugged his shoulders. "You're clairvoyant."

"Poppycock. You're just transparent. Always have been. But out with it. What's been going on?"

"Thomas Bennington, Sr. of Bennington and Bennington Enterprises in Dallas is my grandfather. And, Sherise…my friend Cooper says they're one of the wealthiest families in Dallas."

"No way!" Sherise said, eyebrows raised. "Have you met him?"

"Sure have. I've seen him in person twice. At first he denied the possibility, but then he asked me to take a DNA test. Of course I agreed. It was a slam-dunk. Ninety-nine point nine percent certainty."

"Well, I'll be…" She shook her head. "What does he look like?"

Lucas searched his mind for a few moments for a fitting image. "Like the guy on the Monopoly board…without the top hat."

"That's pretty descriptive, all right." She chuckled. "And your father?"

"He doesn't know where Everett is. Says he's been gone over twenty years. Just dropped off the face of the earth, it seems."

The door opened and Tina entered with the tea and potpie. "Thanks, Tina," Sherise said. "Would you close the door on your way out?"

"I'm going to find him," Lucas said when he and Sherise were alone again. "I have to."

"And your mother?"

"I have to find her too, but for an entirely different reason. She's listed in the will as one-third owner of the estate, so I can't do anything until I at least make a genuine effort to locate her. One that will satisfy the judge." Lucas dug into his lunch and washed the bite down with a long swig of sweet tea.

"I assume you've talked to Isabel."

"She says she doesn't know where Carmen is, but I don't believe her. Just by the way she acted...it seemed like she *did* know something. Said Carmen doesn't want to be found. How does she know if she's not in contact with her?"

"So you have the names of both of your biological parents, but no one seems to know where they are. I don't buy that for a second. You just haven't talked to the right people."

"Who *are* the right people?" Lucas asked with exasperation. "Thomas Bennington, Sr. doesn't know where Everett Bennington is. Or so he says. Isabel doesn't know where Carmen is. Or so she says. What's my next step?"

"I have no clue." Sherise patted his shoulder. "But let's put our thinking caps on."

"I guess I could hire a private detective, but I'll bet Mr. Bennington has already tried that. With all that money, what would stop him?"

"Unless..."

"Unless what?"

"Unless he wanted to let sleeping dogs lie. What if he knew about Everett and Carmen and didn't want that little snippet about a member of his family to hit the papers?"

"Oh, Sherise. I'm no closer to finding my father than I was when I first saw his name on my birth certificate. At this point it's really more important that I find my mother. I need to start probating the will. I know it doesn't have to be done immediately, but I don't want it hanging over my head forever."

"Do you want my advice?" Sherise asked and Lucas nodded. "Don't give up on Isabel. I've always thought she knew something about Carmen."

"Yeah. I might have to pay her a visit soon and try a little harder to get it out of her. It'll probably make her mad, but that's obviously no loss to me."

Chapter Fifteen

Digging way back in his memory, Lucas recalled that although Isabel never paid much attention to him, she seemed to like Maria. His aunt was thirteen years older than they were, and for that reason their parents paid her to babysit whenever the elder Avilas and Vargases went out for a night on the town.

When the three of them were alone, Isabel spent most of her time showing Maria how to put on makeup, braiding her hair, and talking to her about boys Isabel was currently flirting with at school. Lucas was virtually ignored. And this gave him an idea.

What if he told Maria everything and enlisted her help in persuading his aunt to spill the beans about Carmen? Would she be a willing participant? Or would it sully his chances with Maria if she thought he shouldn't try to manipulate Isabel?

There was only one way to find out, but he would broach the subject gently. His walk back home from the town square had afforded him plenty of time to mull this strategy. He knew she had choir practice every Saturday at three and would wait until later that evening to call her. Meanwhile, there was still plenty to do in the garage and staying busy would help the time pass faster.

Lucas glanced at his watch, eager to make a phone call…but with ambivalent feelings about involving his neighbor in his situation. She answered on the first ring. "Hi, Lucas. I was just thinking about you."

His heart grew a bit more noticeable in his chest. "You were?"

"Yeah. I wondered if you wanted to talk some more about the plans for Sherise's party. Or do you have too much to do?"

"I'm kind of at a standstill right now. I was thinking about grilling some burgers tonight. Want to join me?" The chicken fried steak from Sherise's would have to wait till tomorrow.

"Only if I can bring this potato salad that's been in my fridge for a couple of days."

"No objection from me. Mustard, I hope."

"Of course! Is there any other kind?"

"How does six o'clock sound? Too soon?"

"No. I can be there by then."

The thought of seeing Maria again so soon made Lucas smile…and wonder what he should wear. She seemed to go for more casual clothes, so he'd put on a pair of khaki shorts and a navy T-shirt. *It is, after all, a cookout. Don't want to overdress like I did for the lake.*

"I smelled those burgers before I was all the way across the street." Maria sat the bowl of potato salad on the table and tossed her house key and phone down beside it.

"How do you feel about eating in the backyard?" Lucas asked.

"The more I can do outside, the better I like it. A carryover from playing outside when we were kids, I guess. What can I do to help with setup?"

"Take a look out back. Maybe I was being presumptuous, but I felt fairly confident you'd want to eat out there."

"Whoa! Tablecloth, flowers and everything. I'm impressed." Impressed by more than the table. He really did look good, Maria thought, with his sandy brown hair just slightly tousled and that signature crooked grin on his face.

"If we're going to have a picnic, it might as well be a nice one. And the weather's perfect. We need to take advantage of it before triple digits set in."

They worked in tandem carrying drinks and trays from the kitchen to the picnic table. "I remember this table," Maria said, running her fingers over the shellacked wooden bench seat. "You've had it a long time, haven't you?"

"Yeah. I actually think your dad might have helped Papa Joe make it."

"Well, then, it's extra special that we're eating out here."

"I know we need to talk about Sherise's party…and I have some ideas, but I also have a favor to ask. Which first?" Lucas asked as he handed her the platter of burgers fresh from the grill.

"I'm eager to hear about your ideas for the party, but you've piqued my curiosity so let's go with the favor first."

"Okay. Do you remember when we were kids and Isabel would babysit us when our parents would go out together?"

"Yeah. I saw her a few times when Rosa was sick. She came mostly at night when the hospice nurses weren't here. We didn't talk much though. Why do you ask?"

"Remember when she used to braid your hair and put lipstick on you and dress you up in her old princess dresses?"

"Vaguely. But you seem to remember more than I do. I'm still wondering what this is leading to."

"I always thought she liked you more than she liked me. I wasn't wrong, was I?"

"I don't know. I never thought about it. Lucas, this conversation is getting more mysterious by the minute. What are you trying to say?"

"I have a feeling she knows where my mother is and I need to find her now…because she's in the will. Or Isabel at least knows something about her that might help me find her. She won't tell me, though. I thought she might tell you if you asked her." He held up crossed fingers on both hands.

"Yeah…" Maria hesitated. "I don't know. That was a long time ago. I don't think she likes me as much now as she used to. And I don't think it would help your cause if she thought I was butting in."

Lucas sighed, reached for the potato salad, and scooped a large portion for his plate. "You're probably right. I'm sorry. Forget I said anything. I'm sure you don't want to get involved, and I understand. Let's talk about the party."

Maria suspected she'd disappointed Lucas, but he seemed to have accepted it—on the surface anyway—so she moved on too. "You said you had some ideas?"

"Do you have a venue yet? You mentioned the fellowship hall at your church. Is that a done deal?"

"I haven't asked Paul yet, but the more I think about it, the more I think it's too small. Do you have something in mind?"

"I was thinking a barn might be fun, but I can't think of anyone who has one that would work."

"Oh my goodness! Lucas! You're a genius! Kacie has two barns on her ranch, and I think one is only used for storing hay. I'll bet she would let us use that one. We might have to clean it out, though. Or at least move the hay bales against the walls."

"Unless there's a lot of big, heavy equipment in there too, that wouldn't be a problem. I could round up some guys from high school who still live around here. We could get that done in a couple of hours. Have you thought any more about entertainment?"

"I've called around to find a DJ but no luck. Do you know one?" Maria asked. "Maybe someone you went to school with who wouldn't cost an arm and a leg?"

"What about live music? Have you heard of a local band called the Red Hill Boys? I went to school with a couple of them. One of my friends plays the steel guitar. I think Sherise would enjoy that if they're available. And I think I could appeal to their sense of community. Besides, it would be good publicity for them. They do mostly country, but I'll bet they could slip in some Motown. What do you think?"

"In a barn. With a local band. I love it! Sherise will love it! And as Rob Vargas says, 'Is it even country if there's no steel guitar?' Do you think we can pull it off?"

"You ask your friend about the barn, and I'll call the guys I know in the band."

Maria had left her phone in the kitchen but heard it ring through the screen door. "I'd better see who it is."

"Sure."

It was her pastor. She listened as he talked, while sneaking a peek at the broad expanse of Lucas's back through the open door. "I can do that. In fact, I'd love to. When?... Next Saturday morning, leaving the church at nine?... I'll put it on my calendar. Thanks for inviting me."

"Everything okay?" Lucas asked when she returned.

"That was Paul Carpenter from my church inviting me to go with the group to feed the homeless in Dallas next Saturday," she explained to him. "I've gone with them a couple of times before, but this time he wants me to bring my guitar and sing a few songs. Should be fun, but it's sad too, in a way."

"I can imagine. I see them when I go downtown to the courthouse, but I've never had a desire to talk to any of them. Takes a special kind of person to do that. I've often wondered how many can't help being there and how many want to be there because it's the easy way out. People give them things and they don't have to work or engage in society."

His comments came as a shock to Maria, and she felt an invisible wall go up between them. "Lucas! Do you really feel that way?"

"If I'm being honest, yes. I've been told many of them won't go to shelters because they have to work—in the kitchen or whatever—to earn the right to stay there. And I imagine many of them couldn't pass the drug tests. So they take the easy way out and stay on the street."

She bristled. "You think living on the street is easy?"

"In some ways. I'm sure there are some who can't help it and are just down on their luck. But it's probably hard to tell them apart. I don't want to put a damper on it for you, though."

A sudden chill lingered in the air between them, and the rest of the meal was a blur for Maria. She'd never seen this side of Lucas. It took her by surprise and didn't leave her with pleasant thoughts. She wondered if he'd always felt this way or if law school and being an attorney had changed him. Maybe they could pick up this conversation later, but now she just wanted to change the subject and try to forget that the sweet little boy she used to know could feel this unsympathetic toward a certain group of people.

"I'd better go now," she said after a few more minutes of party-planning talk. "I have a couple of things to do to get ready to lead the singing at church tomorrow. Thanks for the burgers." She began picking up plates and silverware.

"Leave it," Lucas said. "I have plenty of time."

The sun had set and twilight had brought out a few fireflies. Watching their luminescence switch on and off gave Maria a sad, nostalgic feeling, as if something in her and Lucas's relationship—or whatever it might have been—had just switched off. She thanked him again, swallowed the lump in her throat, and headed across the street to her dark, empty house.

Chapter Sixteen

Thomas Bennington, Sr. wasn't halfway through his first cup of coffee on Monday morning when Max McBride burst through his office door unannounced, with Karen Blaine right on his heels. "I told him I would ask if you wanted to see him this morning, but he wouldn't stop. I'm sorry, Mr. Bennington."

"That's okay, Miss Blaine. I'll see him now. Please close the door on your way out."

"See you later, sarge," Max saluted and called after her as she tossed her head back and huffed out of the office.

"Well, Max, you want to tell me what's so important that you couldn't even give my assistant the courtesy of letting her announce you?"

"Who've you known longer, Mr. B? And who do you trust more? Blaine's on a power trip, and someone needs to put her in her place every once in a while. Might as well be me…since I enjoy it so much."

"So why are you here…other than to annoy my staff?"

"A thought crossed my mind over the weekend, boss, and I couldn't shake it." He unwrapped a mint from the bowl Thomas had kept on his desk since his grandchildren were little.

"Out with it."

"What if Everett doesn't know he has a child? Or knows but has no idea who or where that child is? What if that revelation or discovery could be the catalyst that would turn his life around? Make him want to rejoin society. Get to know his son. Get a job. Find a place to live. He's not like some of the others, Mr. B. He's not an addict. He's not a mental case. He's smart. He's clean. I think he could transition back into society fairly easily…if he had an incentive. Some motivation. Maybe Lucas Avila is exactly what he needs. I haven't met the young man, of course, but from all I could find out about him, he's a son any father would be proud of. What do you think? Shouldn't they have a chance to get acquainted?"

Thomas leaned back in his chair, closed his eyes, and clasped his hands over his stomach. "Why'd you have to hit me with this so early on a Monday morning?" He sat like that for what seemed an eternity to Max and then picked up his desk phone and punched a button. "Karen, bring us two cups of hot black coffee."

Max started to protest. "Thanks, boss, but I've al—"

"You'll need another cup when you hear what I'm going to ask you to do."

Mondays had become Maria's favorite day of the week at school since that was the only day she and her friend Kacie had the same planning period. Maria would arrive early and hurriedly get the music ready for her classes, make a fresh pot of coffee in the teachers' lounge, and take two steaming cups to Kacie's room. Sometimes she helped her friend get her classroom ready for the day, and sometimes, if Kacie had worked late on Friday, they had time to sit and enjoy a few moments of peace and quiet before their students started arriving.

Maria hoped Kacie didn't have much to do today because there were so many things she needed to talk about. She found her friend sitting at her desk grading papers and sat the two mugs of coffee down on the handmade coasters that had been a Christmas present from one of her students. She pulled up the usual chair and offered to help.

"Thanks, but I only have two more. Won't take long. Everything else is ready. I came in and worked part of the day on Saturday."

"I'm sorry you had to do that, Kace. I know you have plenty to do at home."

"Don't be sorry. I enjoy being here with no interruptions. I can get so much done when I'm alone."

"Yeah, I've done that before, but I don't like to make a habit of it." Maria tore open a couple of packets of sugar and poured them into her coffee and stirred. "I really enjoy my weekends."

"You have a lot to keep you busy away from school with choir practice and trips to the lake. How are your parents? I'm guessing you didn't take Lucas back to Cypress Grove, did you?"

Maria stared at the colorful bulletin board across the room for a few seconds before answering. "No, but I did see him a couple of times this weekend. Friday night we went to Uncle Rio's, and Saturday he grilled hamburgers in his backyard."

"Well. When am I going to meet this guy? Sounds promising."

"Definitely not promising…and I'll tell you why in a minute. But first I have something to ask you."

"Okay…" Kacie tilted her head and eyed her friend quizzically.

"Do you remember I told you about the surprise birthday party we're planning for Sherise? This might be too huge of a favor to ask, but..." Maria paused.

"But what?"

"I was wondering if we could have the party in your barn. The small one. The one that has all the hay. It was Lucas's idea. He and some friends would clean it out and then put everything back like it was before."

"Of course! Great idea!" Kacie said without hesitation and clapped both hands on her desk. "That wouldn't be a problem. In fact, I think it would be fun. I could help decorate. Maybe string some sparkly lights. Consider it a done deal. But wait!" She leaned back in her chair. "We were talking about Lucas and you used the words...I think your exact words were 'definitely not promising.' What's going on? That doesn't sound like the Maria from last week. And you said you saw him twice over the weekend. What happened?"

"While I was at his house Saturday night, Paul called and invited me to go with the group from church to feed the homeless next Saturday. And he wants me to bring my guitar this time. Of course I'm going. I'm looking forward to it."

"So what's the problem?"

Maria hesitated for a moment before she dislodged the knot in her throat and found her voice. "We started talking about the homeless people, and Lucas seems to have quite a distaste for them. He tries to avoid them whenever he has to go downtown to the courthouse. I'm just not sure I could be interested in someone who feels that way." She shrugged. "You know?"

Kacie's expression was sympathetic. "I do know. That mindset is so foreign to my sweet friend who actually brakes for butterflies. You're such a tenderhearted soul. And you need someone who understands that and feels the same way, right?"

"I like Lucas, but I don't think that's something I can overlook."

"I understand, but that's too bad because I thought you were really getting into him."

"I was. He has a lot of good qualities, but this is important to me. A guy I date needs to feel the same way I do about the worth of all people...regardless of their situation in life."

"People can change," Kacie suggested. "Why don't you ask him to go with you?"

"I don't think so, Kace. I don't think he'd go...and if he did, I'm not sure how he would react to them. It's a different world down there."

"I'm sure."

Maria pulled her phone out of her pocket and glanced at the time. "I'd better go and get a few things ready for the fifth graders. We're starting to learn a new song today. It's fun, but a challenge at the same time. See you at lunch." She made her way down the hall to the music room, thinking about Lucas the whole way...until she heard the happy chatter and saw the kinetic energy of the children bounding through the door.

Their exuberance about her class always made her day, but today that niggling thought about Lucas in the back of her mind put a damper on her enthusiasm.

Tuesday morning started earlier than most mornings for Max McBride. He had to locate someone for his boss—he felt sure he could do that—and make preparations for an important meeting. One that could change the trajectory of not one, not two, but potentially three lives. Thomas Bennington had tasked him with finding Carmen Avila and getting the story of her relationship with his son. Then, if Max and his boss thought it appropriate, he would see if she was amenable to talking with Lucas and possibly

Everett. It was a huge ask by Mr. Bennington, but Max had been involved in even more difficult and volatile dealings for his boss.

Thomas had wanted to stay out of it. He was afraid his involvement would hit the papers and cause embarrassment for his wife and older son. If all went well, however, he thought he might want to talk to Everett if he was willing. It was a long shot, but if he didn't take it, he'd never know.

A lot was riding on Max's finding Carmen and he didn't take it lightly. He'd worked for Mr. B for more than twenty years, and to date this was the most important thing his boss had asked of him. Max had always thought Everett dropped out of society because of PTSD caused by the Gulf War. Now he wasn't so sure. A couple of other possibilities kept floating across his mind. Did Carmen get pregnant and vanish without telling Everett about her condition? Did she tell him she was pregnant and then leave for some reason? Had Everett tried to get her to have an abortion?

Max and Thomas both realized Carmen was the key, and she would be the one to unlock the mystery of the newest member of the Bennington family. Max knew it was more difficult to find a woman who could have married and changed her name, but he'd solved more difficult problems since he'd been on retainer with Mr. Bennington.

Finding Everett was one of them. In fact, it took him over a year, but he'd been determined and his persistence paid off. In the fifteen plus years he'd been keeping an eye on him, Max had grown rather fond of Thomas's younger son. Knew his habits and thought him to be a fine man with a good character. But as long as he seemed content in Dallas's homeless community, both Max and Everett's father didn't see any need to intervene.

Now, though, things were different. A son was in the picture—along with a probable romantic relationship—

and the detective was just curious enough to want to solve this mystery as quickly as he could. Not only for his boss's sake, but for his too. The air of mystery surrounding a man who could have stayed in one of the wealthiest families in Dallas but chose to go in the opposite direction had always intrigued Max McBride, and now he had a chance of possibly cracking that riddle.

He hopped in his red BMW, pushed a button to lower the roof, and drove straight to the eight-story Dallas County Records Building between Elm and Main Streets, zipping past most of the other cars on the highway and letting the spring wind blow through what little hair he had left. The parking garage was always full, but he managed to squeeze into the one remaining tight space. Time would tell how much information he could find on such a common name as Carmen Avila, especially when he didn't know if she'd ever married. He had her Trinity Springs background, a picture from an online high school yearbook, and an approximate age, but other than that, it was going to be like looking for a needle in a haystack.

Chapter Seventeen

On Saturday morning the weather was overcast and gloomy, a perfect fit for Maria's mood. She hadn't been able to kick disappointing thoughts of Lucas all week, and today she would serve and sing for the people he found so objectionable. As she had practiced a few hymns last night, she'd felt unexpected tears well up behind her eyelids at the thought of what might have been.

From the day Lucas had returned to Trinity Springs and Maria knocked on his front door and eyed an all-grown-up Lucas with that sandy brown hair and that crooked grin, she couldn't ignore the attraction she'd felt. She'd had hopes of a possible budding relationship, but that seemed unlikely now, and it made her sad. Sad, not only for her, but for Lucas too. She so desired him to see the value in all people, but she felt nothing she could say would change his mind.

After showering and donning jeans and a T-shirt, she pulled her hair back into a ponytail and applied a little lip gloss. No curling iron or makeup for her today. Keep it simple.

She dropped her sheet music and phone in her backpack and grabbed a protein bar and her guitar case. It took all of five minutes to drive from her house to the church where she would get in the van that would take eight people into Dallas for the day. Five minutes. One of the perks of living in a small town.

Before she'd left her house, she'd noticed Lucas's car in the driveway across the street, but he hadn't called last night, and of course, she hadn't called him. She had, however, texted him in the middle of the week to tell him they would be able to use Kacie's barn for the party, and he texted her back to say the Red Hill Boys offered to play at no charge. Things were coming together—for the party anyway.

Pastor Paul and a couple of other guys had the food and hygiene supplies packed when she arrived. Paul's wife Cathy didn't always go with the group, but today she was already on the van. Maria climbed in beside her. "I'm glad you're going today. It's been a while since I've been down there, so I might need some guidance," Maria said.

"Honestly, it's like riding a bicycle. Just listen to what your heart tells you to do. They just want to be treated like human beings instead of animals. Don't be afraid to shake a hand or give a pat on the back. And they're gonna *love* your music. After you've done a few songs—if you feel comfortable—you might want to throw it open to requests. But that's up to you."

"I could do that. If it's something I've heard at least a few times, I can probably pick it out."

"And if it's something you don't know, don't be afraid to say so. We'll eat first. You can help me put tablecloths and food on the tables after the guys set them up."

"I'm glad Paul asked me to do this."

"I sometimes wonder who gets the most out of it," Cathy said, "the homeless or those of us who attempt to serve them. Paul has been coming down here for several years and has developed relationships with some of the guys…especially the veterans. Did you know we lost a son in Iraq?"

"I do remember hearing that, and I'm so sorry, Cathy."

"I think he feels that when he's helping these guys he's doing it for Logan."

"Of course. That would make it so personal and meaningful."

Maria and Cathy sat in comfortable silence as the church van ate up the miles on the highway. Fields of wildflowers dotted the scenery until they were replaced by automobile dealerships, strip malls, and restaurants as the van neared Dallas. A fitting metaphor, Maria thought.

By the time they were approaching the Dallas city limits, it had become one of those spring days in Texas that approached near perfection. The clouds had broken, and the sun was peeking out here and there. High sixties, with just enough of a nip in the air to render the air conditioner unnecessary with the windows slightly lowered. Maria hoped the people would take advantage of prime weather conditions and turn out in droves. They had tons of food, and she knew Paul had prepared a short, uplifting message to share with them after the meal and before the music.

The last time she'd been downtown there'd been a good turnout—and the weather wasn't this conducive to sticking around—so she had high hopes for today. She'd prepared three songs: "Days of Elijah," "Amazing Grace (My Chains Are Gone)," and "How Great Thou Art." Then she'd throw it open for requests as Cathy suggested. She hoped they wouldn't be shy but would sing along and shout out some requests, but since this was the first time she'd brought her guitar, Maria didn't know what to expect.

As they entered Dallas proper, so many of the buildings and landmarks brought back memories. She had, after all, grown up here. She'd learned to drive on these streets, these highways. The tollway took them straight into downtown, and the van maneuvered around the one-way streets until they were in the area where they would set up for the meal. A large crowd had already gathered, and as Paul and some of the men exited the van, many handshakes and pats on the back were given freely. It was evident that trusted relationships had evolved over the years.

Some of the men from the community pitched in to help set up tables, while others stood around and watched. Paul called many of them by name. "Good to see you, Carl." "Hey, Dave!" "Long time no see, Marty." "Shane, could I get you and Benny to help the ladies put the food on the table?"

The majority of the attendees were men, but a few women and even some children showed up. Maria didn't like to think about children being homeless. That fact raised all sorts of questions in her mind, not the least of which was whether they were able to attend school. Her heart hurt thinking that might not be the case. All children, regardless of their circumstances, should have access to an education.

Maria had been wondering if some in the crowd would leave after the meal and the message, but as far as she could see, everyone was hanging around. Paul got down from the tall stool he'd been perched on and indicated for Maria to climb up, so she slipped her guitar strap over her head and took her place in the spotlight. She didn't usually get nervous when she sang, but today she wanted it to go well and there were a few butterflies in her stomach as she started. They dissipated, however, as she rounded the corner from the first song to the second. And by the time she started the third, she was in her groove and going strong. A few people who knew the songs had begun to sing along with her.

At the end of her set, a guy in the front asked for "What a Friend We Have in Jesus," and Maria was happy to oblige with a couple of verses. When that song was over and she didn't see any more hands in the air, she began to get down from her perch and remove her guitar strap when she heard Paul's voice. "I see a hand in the back. Maria, could you wait just a minute and let's see what Benny wants to hear?"

The man in the back spoke softly. "Does it have to be religious?"

"No. It certainly doesn't," Maria said. "What would you like to hear?"

"Do you know any George Jones?"

"Maybe. My dad likes him. Try me."

"Do you know 'He Stopped Loving Her Today'?"

"I think so…but you might have to help me. That okay? Benny, right?"

He nodded slightly.

"Well, Benny, I obviously don't have a steel guitar, but let's see what this Martin will do. You sing along and keep me on track."

Maria played an intro and when she began the song, his resonant voice picked up the lyrics. He sang the first line softly and tentatively. Maria played a little louder. He sang the second line with more feeling. Maria was enthralled with his voice. She could close her eyes and picture Alan Jackson singing the song at Jones's funeral service. Benny sang until he got to the speaking part and stopped. She couldn't completely see his face, but she suspected he was choked up. She'd wondered a couple of times if he would make it through the song.

"Thank you for helping me, Benny. And thanks for suggesting that one. I really like it," she said. "I think it's time to go, but thank you all for coming out and for being a great audience. I look forward to playing for you again."

Applause started softly and grew in intensity. She hopped down from the stool and gave a slight bow. *What a rush*, she thought. *This is the most fun I've had playing for anyone in a long time.*

Paul and Cathy came over and Cathy gave her a hug. "You were so good! They loved it."

"I had a good time. What's the deal with Benny? He has an amazing voice. And his singing was so emotive. It almost seemed personal."

Paul piped up. "He's quite a guy. A little on the shy side, though. Doesn't talk much. I was surprised he sang. Actually, I was surprised he even suggested a song. We'd better go, though, if I'm going to get you home in time for choir practice."

Maria spotted Benny again as he and some of the other guys were helping to collapse the tables and put them in the trailer. Their eyes met and she smiled. His eyes eased into a smile that finally reached one side of his mouth, and that crooked grin looked familiar to her for some reason. He had the lightest blue eyes she'd ever seen. In fact, it looked as though God had added a tiny drop of white in with the blue when he mixed the colors for them. His hair was a sandy blond, his skin tan, and Maria imagined he must have been quite the heartthrob in his younger years.

All the way home Maria couldn't get one thought out of her mind: the stories behind the people she'd seen today. Each person had a different reason for living on the street. She knew some had recently lost jobs and couldn't afford rent, but some had been there for many years. Cathy told her that Benny was one of those. Cathy didn't know exactly how long, but she assumed it was at least fifteen or twenty years. Maybe more. What had caused him to stay that long? Had the war done that much of a number on him? Would it be possible for him to ever rejoin society?

The thought stayed with her during choir practice, and as she lay in bed that night trying to go to sleep, it was still vying for her attention.

Chapter Eighteen

On Sunday afternoon Maria made a list of names and numbers for Lucas to call to spread the word about Sherise's party. The venue and entertainment were locked in, and Livvy was making calls around town about food. A couple of restaurants and a bakery had already said they would donate. It didn't matter that the restaurants were in direct competition with Sherise's Café. This was a community event.

Maria had thought it would be best if she and Lucas didn't spend much time together, but when she finished the list, she glanced across the street and saw his car was still in the driveway. She rationalized that taking it directly to him would be easier than emailing it, so she strolled over and knocked on the door. He opened it immediately, combing his fingers through his hair, and looking better than he should in jeans and a white polo shirt.

But for Maria looks went only so far. She had to be able to respect a guy to be really interested, and Lucas had said some things that caused her to have second thoughts.

"Maria. Hi. Come in. You must have read my mind." He opened the door wider and she stepped inside.

"What do you mean?"

"I've been busy all weekend, but I was just thinking about texting to see if you want to grab a bite to eat before I head back to Dallas."

Determined not to be pulled back into her former state of mind, she blurted out, "I came to give you this list. People to call about the party."

"Okay. Great." He took the list from her. "I'll do that this week." A moment passed and he said, "So do you?"

Maria was staring into space, lost in thought. "I'm sorry. What?"

"Do you want to get something to eat before I have to hit the road?"

She tried, unsuccessfully, to avoid his eyes because they did something to her. Caused an emotion she knew she had to avoid now. But as their eyes locked, she had a little trouble stammering out her answer. "Um… I… I don't think so. I'd better not. I, uh, had a late lunch."

"Okay. Well, I guess I'll see you next weekend then. Are the rest of the plans for the party coming together?"

"Yeah." She hesitated for a minute. Needed to regain her composure. "Would you be able to get some guys together to clean out the barn next Saturday? And then Kacie and I can decorate the morning before the party."

"Sure. What time does it start…and how are you going to get Sherise there without telling her anything?"

"I'm going to cancel choir practice and tell her it's Serve Saturday and this time we're helping Kacie clean out the stalls for the rescue horses. She'll be all over that. The choir members will meet at the church and carpool to the ranch. Tell all the people you call to be there by two forty-five and to carpool if possible and pull their cars around behind the big barn. We'll try to arrive between three fifteen and three twenty. I wrote it all down for you at the bottom of the list."

"Sounds like a plan. I'm glad you're doing this for her."

"*We're* doing this for her. A lot of people will be involved. I hope she's surprised." Maria shifted her weight to the other foot, still uneasy as Lucas's gaze remained on her. "I'd better go…" she said, her words hanging in the air. "Thanks for making the calls." They stood there awkwardly for a moment, and as she backed out the door, she couldn't help noticing the puzzled look on his face.

Back at home Maria felt restless and on edge so she turned on the burner under the kettle, took a bag of chai tea out of her tea caddy, and reached in the cabinet for her favorite mug. As she listened to the hiss of the water slowly coming to a boil, she felt that same agitation in her stomach. Why had she let him affect her so much in such a short time? She usually had a better handle on her emotions than this.

Her first instinct in times like this was usually to call her mother. No. She didn't want to have to go into a lengthy explanation, and her mother would be able to wangle it out of her. But her aversion to being alone when she felt this uneasy got the best of her, and she picked up her phone and dialed.

"Mama?"

"Hi, there. I wondered if you'd be coming out this afternoon."

"No. I just wanted to hear your voice."

"What's wrong?"

"What makes you think something's wrong when I want to hear your voice?"

"Because I know *your* voice, and it's telling me something's wrong."

"I think I will come if it's okay."

"Absolutely. Because if you don't, I'm coming over there."

"Thanks, Mom. Be there soon."

Maria transferred her tea to a to-go cup, added a bit of honey, put a lid on it, and grabbed her purse. She felt better just knowing she would be with her parents in thirty minutes.

Her dad greeted her at the door with a bear hug. "I'd love the company, but I don't think you came over to go fishing with me, did you?"

He could always make his daughter laugh. "Not this time, Daddy. Soon though."

"I know you want to talk to your mama, so I'll give you two some privacy. But remember, if you need me to beat up someone, all you have to do is holler."

"I know you always have my back, but I'm fine. Really."

"I'm glad." He gave her a peck on the cheek. "Livvy, your daughter's here. I'm outta here. I'll be doing a little more planting in the garden until it's time to see if the fish are biting."

"Bye, Daddy. I'll see you again before I go."

"Of course you will," Livvy said. "I'm making tacos for supper. I know you can't turn those down."

"We'll see. I'm not very hungry."

"Sit down while I brown the meat. Want something to drink?"

Maria pulled out a chair at the old oak table around which so many of her teenage problems had been solved. "I had a cup of tea on the way over."

"What's going on, honey?"

"I don't know where to start."

"How are the plans for the party progressing? We're going to have plenty of food, so that's not a concern. You have the venue and entertainment taken care of. What's left?"

"It's not that," Maria said as she twisted her hair around her index finger.

"School?" Livvy prompted again. "Don't keep me guessing here."

"It's Lucas." She took a deep breath and exhaled slowly in an attempt to regain her emotional footing.

"Lucas? Is he okay?"

"He's okay, but I found out last weekend that he basically thinks homeless people are throwaways."

"What? That's hard to believe." Livvy put down the spatula, turned off the burner under the ground beef, and sat down at the table across from her daughter. "You like him more than you were willing to admit to yourself, don't you?"

"I guess I did. But I can't be interested in someone who feels that way. You know I can't."

"Of course I do, but don't count Lucas out yet. He's such a nice young man. Maybe he just hasn't thought through the situation completely."

"Mama, I was at his house when Paul called and asked me to sing for them. That's how the conversation got started, and he said some things that surprised me."

"Like what?" Livvy asked.

"Like most of them want to be there because they're lazy, and it's the easy way out so they won't have to work."

"You do realize, sweetheart, that there's a happy medium between how you see them and how Lucas sees them. Don't you?"

"If you could have been there yesterday… There were kids, too, and the way they ate you'd think they hadn't had a meal in days. Some of the guys pitched in and helped Paul and the others set up the tables. And Mama…"

"Yes?"

"There was this guy. He's a veteran. He requested 'He Stopped Loving Her Today' and sang along as I played. I wish you could have heard him. It was beautiful. And it really got to me for some reason."

"Do you know anything about his situation?"

"Just that he was in Desert Storm, and Paul thinks he might have PTSD. How can we send our men and women off to fight for us and then treat them like they don't matter when they come back bruised and battered—if not physically, then emotionally?"

"It's not right, but that's a discussion for another time. Back to why you came over this afternoon. Don't give up on Lucas. He's a good boy. I know Joe and Rosa raised him right. Maybe if you talked with him and told him some of the stories about the people you interacted with…" Livvy reached across the table to squeeze her daughter's hand.

"I'm okay, Mama. You can finish browning the meat. What can I do to help with the tacos? I think I *will* stay and eat with y'all."

"Good. How about grating some cheese? But don't think for a minute it escaped me that you're ignoring my suggestion to talk to Lucas."

"I don't know, Mama. He sounded so…so…callous. How can he just write off a whole group of people when he doesn't know their stories?"

"How can you defend them when you don't know their stories? I'm glad I have a tenderhearted daughter, but sometimes your best characteristic can be your worst characteristic. Or at least the one that keeps you from recognizing the truth sometimes. I'm fully behind what Pastor Paul does, but I'll bet even he knows they don't all want to better their station in life. No group is all good or all bad. We can't stereotype people. We have to look at them as individuals."

"You're probably right. Maybe I've been a little delusional about the whole thing. Maybe Lucas is the one who's being realistic."

"As I said before, there's usually a happy medium to every difficult situation. We just have to learn how to meet somewhere in the middle. Don't write Lucas off. Try to find out why he feels the way he does."

What was it about being with her parents that could calm Maria so quickly? The problem didn't have to be solved totally. Just laying it out there and knowing they would be there for her no matter what was worth more than silver and gold. But she had to admit her mother did have a point. If she wouldn't look down on someone living on the street, why should she give up on Lucas until she knew why he felt the way he did?

Chapter Nineteen

As Lucas sat in his office on Monday morning, he began to think he'd made a mistake in deciding to keep the house in Trinity Springs. Something was going on with Maria, but he couldn't quite put his finger on it. He'd never been good at reading women, and the few he'd gone out with since leaving home for college had baffled him so much that he'd given up after two or three dates.

He'd thought Maria was different, though. From the time they'd spent together in the last few weeks, she seemed to be open and transparent, straightforward and easy-to-read. But now... Something had changed, and he had racked his brain trying to figure out what it was.

She'd seemed glad when he told her he was planning to keep the house. So that wasn't it. She'd asked him to help plan Sherise's party and liked his ideas of live music in a barn. That wasn't it. When did her attitude change, and why, he wondered. She, like the others, was becoming an enigma.

As he sat at his desk thinking about how quickly a person's life could change without warning, Cooper entered his office to remind him they were due in court in an hour. It usually took about twenty minutes to get downtown from Benson and Hughes law offices, but they always left early to allow for traffic, parking, and slow elevators. The judge they'd drawn for this case didn't take kindly to tardiness, so it was time to head out.

"Want to ride with me, or will you need your car before coming back to the office?" Cooper asked his friend.

"We'll have better luck finding one parking spot instead of two. Want me to drive, though?"

"I will. You're going to wear out your car going back and forth to Trinity Springs every weekend. You're not still cleaning out the house, are you? Have you asked her out yet?" A sly grin spread across Cooper's face.

"I'll tell you what's going on when we're in the car." Lucas put his laptop, a couple of file folders, and a yellow legal pad in his messenger bag and slung the strap over his head. "Let's roll."

The sunlight glinted through the windshield as Cooper MacDonald threaded his silver Audi through heavier-than-usual tollway traffic, and Lucas plucked his sunglasses out of his inside coat pocket.

"Spill it. The Coop is all ears. Have you asked her out or not?"

"Score one for *not*."

"What is wrong with you? Saving her for me? And if that's the case, I approve. That is, if she really *is* hot."

"Oh, she's hot all right, but I don't know, Coop. Something was different this time."

"What do you mean?"

"She wasn't the same easy-going, fun Maria she'd been before. Seemed distant and aloof. Just not like it had been between us."

"Maybe she expected you to ask her out, and when you didn't…"

That was something Lucas hadn't thought of, but he considered it for a moment before he said, "I don't think that's it. I asked her if she wanted to get a bite to eat last night before I had to head back, and she said no. But I don't think she had anything else to do. I'll never be able to figure out women."

"It's not that hard, man. They just want to be treated like queens, but they don't want you to act like a king. That's the long and short of it right there." Cooper laughed at his declaration, but Lucas failed to see the humor. After all, Cooper didn't know Maria and he did.

"Maria's not like that," he protested.

"Ha! All women are like that. What makes her different?"

"Well, for one thing, she's always doing things for other people…like this birthday party for Sherise. And she helps to feed and sing for the homeless down here. She came down with her church group Saturday."

"How'd it go?"

"I don't know. Okay, I guess. I didn't ask her."

"Say what? You knew she was doing that, and she *knew* you knew she was doing that, and you didn't ask her how it went? Didn't give her a chance to talk about it?"

"I didn't think about it."

"Rule number two. In addition to being treated like a queen, women like to talk about things. You know. Feelings and stuff. You need to fix this, my friend. That is, if you care enough to put in some work."

"She's pretty special," Lucas admitted.

"Then I think you know what you need to do. She doesn't happen to have a hot friend, does she?"

"She's mentioned someone she teaches with who lives on a ranch, but I haven't met her."

"A cowgirl, huh? That could be pretty appealing."

At the last minute, the company Lucas and Cooper were representing decided to settle out-of-court, so that left them some time to have a long lunch break before heading back to the office. Lucas didn't take lightly what his friend had said about the situation with Maria. Maybe he had been self-absorbed when he failed to ask about her trip to Dallas on Saturday. Even though they might not see eye-to-eye about people who lived on the street, she deserved to have a chance to talk about her day. After all, she'd seemed happy about the opportunity when her pastor called. That was a point of contention he was going to remedy as soon as he saw her again. And maybe he *had* come across too negative in that conversation. Her conviction about the value of the people on the street gave him something to think about.

Max McBride hadn't had any luck locating Carmen Avila, or whatever her last name might be now. If only he had a current photo of her. The most recent one he could find was at least thirty years old—her senior picture in the Trinity Springs High School yearbook. People changed a lot from age eighteen to almost fifty. Goodness knew he had. Her coal-black hair could be completely gray, or at least partially gray.

Her eyes wouldn't have changed colors, but she could wear glasses now. And if she was anything like a lot of people whose looks evolved, or devolved perhaps, she could have gained a lot of weight. Age tended to do that to some people.

There was one card he hadn't played yet, though. She had a sister who apparently still lived in Trinity Springs. It was possible they'd kept in touch. But how was he going to get any information out of her and still keep the reason for the investigation quiet? He didn't know this Isabel person, but he did know that most people could be motivated by money.

He wouldn't have to mention his boss. In fact, he could even declare a fabricated reason to be looking for her. Carmen was about his age. He would tell her sister he'd met her many years ago in Dallas and lost touch. Just like to meet her for coffee or lunch and catch up. It would be easier to find an Isabel Avila in Trinity Springs than a Carmen Avila in Dallas. Game on!

Chapter Twenty

Lucas could hardly wait to see Maria on Friday and put things right between them. At least he hoped he could. The more he thought about his conversation with Cooper, the more he was convinced his attitude toward the homeless and his failure to show an interest in what she was so passionate about had erected the wall that was now between them. The realization wasn't a pleasant one. It would mean he needed to give his mindset a possible overhaul. At least give a consideration to a different way of thinking. And he needed to hear, really hear, what she had to say about her day in Dallas.

But he had another task to complete before he saw her Friday, so he might as well start now. He took her list out of his bag and began to see how many calls he could make before nine o'clock. She would be impressed if he'd contacted all the people and handed her a completed list.

When Lucas had contacted about half of the names, he decided to go for a run. He needed to move his body and clear his head before he tackled the other half and the paperwork he'd brought home from the office. His job was a little too sedentary for his liking, but at least his apartment was in a neighborhood with a park that was conducive to walking and running. The path encircled a small lake with a fountain in the middle and had been one of the selling points when he was apartment hunting. He'd thought the sun setting on the other side of the lake was pretty spectacular, but now that he'd seen a sunset on Cypress Grove Lake, he was convinced this one paled in comparison. He'd timed it just right tonight though, and because of magnificent cloud formations, it succeeded in making his run more enjoyable as he watched the water turn from blue to gold.

As he felt his body relaxing and his mind clearing, it became obvious to him that he shouldn't wait until the weekend to talk with Maria. No, he'd make a quick trip to Trinity Springs on Wednesday after work. That way, they would be free to clean out the barn and finish planning Sherise's party Saturday without this whatever-it-was hanging over their heads.

On Tuesday evening at seven o'clock, Isabel Avila heard the crunch of gravel outside the small garage apartment she'd occupied for almost twenty years. She peered out the window and watched as a man she didn't recognize climbed the stairs and stood on the landing for a moment until she heard a light *tap tap tap* on the locked and bolted door.

"What?" she yelled without undoing the locks.

He had nothing else to do but to yell back through an unopened door. "Are you Isabel Avila?"

"Who wants to know?"

"My name is Max Kincade, and I'm looking for a Carmen Avila, who I think might be your sister. Am I right?"

She didn't have to give it much thought to assume her nephew was behind this. "Did Lucas send you?"

"Who? May I come in? Or would you step outside for a minute so we can talk more easily than shouting through a door?"

"Yeah. I'll come outside. Just a minute." She ambled over and picked up the .22 she kept by the bed in her tiny studio apartment. If he wanted to talk badly enough, he wouldn't mind looking down the barrel of a rifle while he said his piece.

"Whoa! I don't want any trouble." Max took a couple of steps back and lifted both hands when she stepped out onto the landing. "If you want me off your property, just say so. I'm only trying to locate someone, but it's not important enough to get shot to smithereens."

"Did Lucas send you?" She flipped her ponytail and brushed her bangs out of her eyes.

"Who's Lucas?" he asked.

"Okay. Let me ask it this way then," Isabel said with a sigh as she rolled her eyes. "What do you want with Carmen?"

"We met and had a couple of dates several years ago, but I moved away and we lost touch. She might not even remember me. I'm back now—still not married—and I'd like to see her again to catch up. Maybe over coffee or lunch. Nothing nefarious, I can assure you. I just haven't met many people in the area since I moved back."

"I don't know where she is." Isabel turned to go back inside.

"Are you sure? I've done really well financially while I've been away. Maybe you'd like to buy yourself a fancy new gun. That one looks pretty old."

She wheeled around to face Max again. "Suits me just fine. Mr. Smith and Mr. Wesson have taken good care of me for many years. And I don't buy your story. Not for one minute. I know Lucas sent you."

"Ma'am, I don't know this Lucas you're referring to, but I'll be about my business if you say you don't know where Carmen is. You have yourself a good evening now."

"I like your car," Isabel blurted when Max was halfway down the stairs.

He stopped in his tracks and turned. "What?"

"I said I like your car. I don't need a new rifle, but I could use a new car. And I'm especially fond of sexy red convertibles."

"You're a hoot." Max was laughing as he climbed back up to the landing. "I think under different circumstances you and I would get along well." He handed her a freshly printed Max Kincade business card with a fictitious company name. "If you happen to hear from your sister or remember anything about where I might find her or decide you do need a new rifle or a new Easter bonnet or something, would you give me a ring? I'm just looking to renew an old acquaintance. That's all. Good evening, Ms. Avila."

Lucas was still working his way through the list Maria had given him when his phone rang and Isabel's name appeared on the screen. *What would she be calling about? It can't be good.* He had his phone on speaker and was in the middle of a call explaining everything about the party to one of his old high school chums, but when Isabel's name showed up, he rushed the conversation, eager to find out what his aunt had to say. He ended the call to his friend and immediately called Isabel. "You called? I was on the phone. What's up?"

"That Max Kincade guy came to see me."

So she was going to play games. Well, he wasn't in the mood. "What are you talking about? What Max Kincade guy?"

"That guy you sent, looking for Carmen. I already told you I don't know where she is. I guess you didn't believe me."

"Well, you can believe me when I say I don't know any Max Kincade. What did he say?"

"He made up some story about knowing her in the past and wanting to get in touch. Even offered to buy me a new rifle if I'd tell him."

"What? You pulled your gun on him?" Lucas roared in laughter, but nothing his aunt did really surprised him. "Good for you, though. I worry about you sometimes…living alone."

"You don't have to worry about *me*. But you might want to worry about that Mr. Kincade if he comes around again. My patience was already beginning to wear thin with him before he left a few minutes ago."

"Isabel, I didn't send him to you. Honest. But this has me concerned. I wonder who he is and why he's looking for Carmen. Especially now when I need to find her to probate the will. Seems like strange timing. Did he leave any information with you? A phone number or anything?"

"I have his business card. Said to call him if I remembered anything."

"Would you give me the number? Hold on a minute and let me get a pen."

Lucas scribbled the name and number on a notepad, unsure of what he was going to do with the information…if anything. Could be a coincidence, he thought. But the timing wouldn't let his mind park there for long. Did Thomas Bennington decide to try to locate Carmen hoping it would lead to Everett? One thing he did know for sure, though. He would never find out by sitting and wondering. So he picked up his phone again and punched in the number Isabel had given him.

Max was on his way back to Dallas when his Max Kincade burner phone rang. *That little filly didn't waste any time getting back in touch. I wonder if she had second thoughts about getting a new rifle.*

He plucked the phone out of the cup holder and answered it. "Max Kincade here. Did you change your mind about the gun?"

"Mr. Kincade?"

A man's voice. What was going on? He'd given the number to only Isabel. Might as well play along. Apparently she'd given it to someone. "Yes."

"This is Lucas Avila. I'm Isabel Avila's attorney. I'm also her nephew."

I know who you are, but I didn't really want to get you involved in this. "What can I do for you, Mr. Avila? Is Ms. Avila going to sue me? She's the one who pulled a gun on me. I should sue her."

"Nobody's talking about suing anybody. I'm just wondering why you want to find Carmen Avila. Isabel didn't buy your story, and I'm not buying it either."

Think fast, Max. Or buy some time. "I'm not prepared to discuss this over the phone. Can you meet with me tomorrow?"

"I have to work tomorrow and have plans for tomorrow evening. I could meet with you Thursday after work. Say five-thirty? I live in North Dallas."

That's even better. It'll give me time to think about what I'm going to say to him. "Works for me," Max said. "Is a restaurant okay? I'm buying."

"That's not necessary, but a restaurant is fine."

"Mauricio's just off the North Dallas Tollway?"

"Yes. I know where that is. I'll see you there at five-thirty on Thursday. How will I know you?" Lucas asked.

"I'll know you. See you then."

"How—"
Click.

◈◈◈

What the heck? Lucas was stunned. *He'll know me?* Then it hit him. This had something to do with Thomas Bennington. It had to. How else would a random stranger looking for his mother know anything about him? Know what he looked like? And just when he thought his life couldn't get more complicated.

Chapter Twenty-One

When Lucas was about twenty minutes north of Dallas on his way to Trinity Springs Wednesday evening, huge raindrops began to splat one-by-one on the windshield of his Toyota. They fell intermittently at first but became more regular and more intense with each mile marker he passed. After another twenty minutes, he was in a steady downpour, and the rain pelted his windshield so hard the large drops almost seemed like hail. He'd been on the road in a hailstorm before and didn't want to replay that nightmare, so he pulled in to a truck stop as soon as he could to wait it out and check the weather app on his phone for radar.

There was no room to get into a covered spot by the pumps, but he parked close to the building's east side since the wind was blowing hard from the west. Radar didn't look promising. He thought it might ease up a little in about five minutes, though, so he ran in to buy a bottle of water and text Maria. He was thankful she'd seemed happy to hear from him when he told her he'd completed all the calls on his list and was coming to Trinity Springs Wednesday evening and wanted to talk to her. "What a coincidence," she'd said. "I want to talk to you, too, so that's great. Don't have dinner first. I'll make lasagna." He didn't know what had precipitated this apparent change in her attitude toward him, but it made his heart happy.

Still…Cooper's words rang in his ears: *Women want to be treated like queens. And they want to talk and for you to listen.* So listen he would. He'd even prepared some questions he thought she might enjoy answering about her day in Dallas.

In a few minutes, the rain had let up a little, but the air had an eerie green cast to it. He'd seen that before and didn't like it. The calm before the storm. But he needed to get to Trinity Springs, so he hopped in his car, and once he was on the highway, he floored it. Fortunately, this part of the road was long, straight, and flat, and there were only a handful of cars in front of him. The rain had slowed enough that visibility was sufficient for driving a few miles over the speed limit. He could almost taste that lasagna already, but mostly he was just hoping Maria was still in as good a mood as she was last night on the phone. After a few more miles, the rain increased in intensity again, and Lucas heard the clink of light hail on the roof of the car.

***

The call came just as Maria was layering the lasagna. "Hey, Lucas. Where are you?"

"I'm about ten minutes from Trinity Springs. It's hailing here. Is it hailing there?"

"Not right now, but we're under a tornado watch. That's the only thing I hate about living in Texas. This unpredictable spring weather."

"I'm going to put my car in the garage, grab an umbrella, and run across the street. Do you need me to bring anything from the house?"

"Maybe some candles and matches—if you have any—in case we lose power. The wind is pretty fierce."

"Okay. See you soon."

Maria had thought she might be nervous about this meeting with Lucas, but she wasn't. In fact, she was looking forward to clearing the air between them. Since the talk with her mother, she'd been willing to give him the benefit of the doubt.

She finished off the layers by sprinkling some grated mozzarella cheese on top, slid the casserole dish into the preheated oven, and set the timer. The loaf of French bread was already sliced and buttered, and dessert was finished, so she turned her attention to finishing the salad that would complete their meal. As she grated carrots and chopped avocados and tomatoes, Maria could feel her anticipation rising. After she tossed the salad with Italian dressing, she put it in the refrigerator, checked her hair and makeup in the mirror, and decided to change tops. She didn't know why. Maybe it was just something to occupy the time while she waited impatiently for the doorbell to ring.

Fifteen minutes later, he splashed through puddles as he sprinted across the street, and Maria opened the door to a drenched Lucas holding a plastic bag full of votive candles. "I couldn't find an umbrella," he mumbled as he stood on the front porch dripping wet.

"Come in," she said laughing. "Let me get you a towel. Looks like you fell into the lake."

"Feels like it, too. I'll stay here until you get that towel. I don't want to get your house wet."

"Don't be silly. You're not going to hurt the house. I'll be right back."

Lucas stepped inside and looked around. He'd been in this house several times when he was very young, but he didn't recognize anything. The décor had Maria written all over it, though. She'd apparently redecorated when she moved in. Dark hardwood floors, pale yellow walls, white sofa and chairs, pink tulips in a vase on a glass coffee table. And the aroma coming from the kitchen. He hoped they would eat soon. He'd worked up quite an appetite navigating through a torrential downpour.

"Here ya go." She handed him a towel and a pair of socks. "I think these might fit you. It can't be comfortable having to suffer wet feet all evening. And I do have a big, fluffy robe that might fit you if you want me to put your slacks and shirt in the dryer. I mean, it's pink, but beggars can't be choosers."

"Now wouldn't I be a sight in a pink robe?" He laughed heartily, glad the comical situation was breaking the ice that had built up between them.

"You're already a sight in wet clothes. So take your pick. Be a sight and uncomfortable all evening…or…be a sight for a little while and then have dry clothes to put back on."

It was logic even an attorney could appreciate. "You make way too much sense. Let me have that robe, and point me to the bathroom."

While Lucas was changing out of his wet clothes and into her bathrobe, the rain and wind returned with a vengeance, and he called to Maria, "Why don't you put the TV on a local station and see what they're saying about this newest weather cell. I just checked radar on my phone, and it doesn't look good."

She flipped on the TV in the kitchen, located a Dallas station, and continued to set dinner on the table. When Lucas appeared adorned in a long pink robe and holding his wet clothes wrapped up in a towel, she almost lost it. "I'm sorry," she said, guffawing at the absolute spectacle standing before her. "I tried really hard not to laugh, but it just wasn't happening."

Fortunately, Lucas was laughing too, and Maria was thankful he was able to see the humor in the situation rather than being embarrassed. She actually thought that said a lot about him and was glad he didn't take himself too seriously.

"Happy to be able to provide the entertainment for the evening," he said, smiling. "Wow! That lasagna smells and looks amazing."

"Let me put those clothes in the dryer and we'll eat."

Just as they were about to sit down at the table, the tornado warning siren wailed and pierced the quiet, startling both of them. Lucas turned up the volume on the TV in time to hear the local weatherman say, "Rotation on the ground has been spotted east of Manville, moving toward Trinity Springs and Cypress Grove Lake. If you live in one of these places or the surrounding area, take shelter in your safe room immediately."

Maria's and Lucas's eyes locked. A mutual understanding. They'd both lived in Texas all their lives and were well aware of what "rotation on the ground" meant. Lucas spoke first. "Do you have an interior room?"

"I always get in my walk-in closet. I keep some pillows and blankets in there."

"Good. Let's grab the food and go."

"I hate this! Why don't they build basements in Texas?"

"We'll be okay," he reassured her. "You go ahead. Point the way and I'll get the stuff and be there in a minute."

"Please hurry! Down the hall and to the right." She grabbed her phone and guitar case and headed for her bedroom.

Lucas's thoughts turned to the possibility of blown out windows and large tree limbs crashing through the roof as he hurriedly filled two plates with lasagna and salad, took them to the closet, and returned for drinks, forks, candles, and matches.

"First things first. I can't wait to dig into this meal," he said, as he sat down cross-legged on the quilt she'd spread out on the closet floor for their impromptu picnic. He looked around and it hit him that he was surrounded by the clothes of a woman he, until a few weeks ago, hadn't thought about in years. Yet, here he was now…delighting in the nearness of her…of her things, her fragrance, her beauty.

"You thought of everything," Maria said. "Even the candles. I wasn't thinking. Just grabbed the first two things I wouldn't want to lose, my phone and guitar."

Lucas willed himself and his thoughts back down to earth. "Your guitar is important to you. I get that. And we could use the flashlights on our phones if the power goes off, but we need to save the battery power to monitor the storm. Candles might come in handy."

"I'm glad you brought the food. I'm starving."

"Me too. Are you still scared?"

"Not as much. I always feel safer in here. And I'm glad you're here."

"Ditto. *Really* glad this didn't happen while I was on the road. Or while the lasagna was still in the oven." He chuckled. Anything to get Maria's mind off the weather and the siren that was still blaring.

"Yeah. Let's eat before it gets cold. Or before the roof blows off. Whichever comes first."

"Hey! I just thought of something. Do you think your parents know to take shelter?"

"Yes. Mama texted me while you were getting the food. They're glad I'm not alone too."

"If you had told me I'd be eating the best lasagna I ever tasted, wearing a pink robe, and sitting on the floor of a closet…well…"

"Lucas! Listen!" She reached out her hand for his.

He'd heard that rumble of impending disaster once before when he was in college and a tornado, sounding just like a train, roared past his dorm. He crawled around the food and sat by Maria, putting his arms around her. She laid her head on his shoulder as tears fell from her eyes onto her pink robe.

"I'm sorry," she said as Lucas felt her body tense. "I just get so scared when it's like this."

"I think the worst is over now, but that's the second time I've been drenched today. I hope you have another robe." He squeezed her tighter and kissed the top of her head…just as the light bulb overhead flickered and went out.

Chapter Twenty-Two

Three heartbeats later, Maria found herself wondering how it would feel to curl up in Lucas's arms like this every night. Just as she was nestling in a little closer, an ear-splitting crack of thunder sounded overhead, and he gently but firmly pushed her over to shield her with his body. Emotions of both fear and anticipation overcame her and tears ran down her cheeks until she could taste their salt with the tip of her tongue. The tornado siren finally quit screaming, but Lucas held on to her for a moment longer, and before he sat up, his lips brushed hers and lingered for a few tantalizing seconds.

Did this count as a kiss, she wondered. *Yes. Yes it did.* And for the first time in her life, Maria was thankful for a storm.

Lucas slowly helped her to a sitting position and started lighting votives. Maria brushed back a couple of small tear-soaked wisps of hair that were stuck to her damp face. Her phone rang, and she felt around on the quilt for it.

"Yes, Mama, the power is out here, too... He's still here." She looked at Lucas and smiled, thinking how incredibly handsome his face was in the candlelight. Not that she hadn't noticed it before, but tonight she saw him with new eyes. "Yeah, we heard it go over the house... I'll tell him, Mama."

"Your parents okay?" Lucas asked when she put her phone down on their makeshift quilt-table.

"Their power is out too, but they're fine. Mama wanted me to tell you thanks for being here. She knows how scared I get with this crazy spring weather."

"Well I, for one, am kind of thankful for the weather today. I hope everyone else is okay, but as for me...I'm better than okay." He reached across and took her hand in his.

The look in his eyes told her as much as his words. She had never appreciated a power outage before, but she was grateful for this one. In the midst of the storm, Lucas's presence made her feel safe, protected. "Me too," she whispered.

"I'm so glad I decided to drive up tonight instead of waiting until Saturday. If I hadn't, I don't know when I would have gotten to model a pink bathrobe...if ever. And I might have to use it to go across the street and find something else to wear back to Dallas. I'm guessing your dryer is electric," he said with a grin.

Maria laughed out loud. "I hadn't thought about your wet clothes still in the dryer. Won't you look cute crossing the street like that? By the way," she said, remembering his call telling her he wanted to come over tonight to talk, "with all that's been going on since you got here, you never told me what you wanted to talk about."

"I wanted to apologize."

She tilted her head and eyed him quizzically. "For what?"

"I didn't even ask when I saw you on Sunday how your visit in Dallas went Saturday. That wasn't very thoughtful of me because I know how much you were looking forward to it."

"That's okay. It was a good day, though. I enjoyed it."

"Want to elaborate? I'd love to hear your thoughts."

"Really?" Maria was surprised but pleased with Lucas's sudden interest in her day in Dallas. Maybe hearing a tornado go over the house had affected him in some way. Whatever it was, she was pleased with this new development.

"Sure," he said. "Tell me about it."

"Okay. Well. It was sad in a way because some of the homeless are families with children, and you can imagine how I feel about that. And some are veterans who risked their lives to fight in wars for our freedoms. Of course, some are there because they're addicted to drugs or mentally unstable. That's heartbreaking too, of course, but I really felt bad for the kids and the veterans. Paul knows them all pretty well, and that helped."

"You sang, right? How did that go?"

"I think they enjoyed it. A couple of people made requests. There was this one guy who sang a George Jones song that he asked me to play. He was pretty impressive. Paul said he's a veteran of Desert Storm and has been on the street a long time."

"Are a lot of them veterans?"

"A few. Not sure how many."

"I guess the trauma of war did a number on some of them."

"Apparently. Did I tell you Paul and Cathy lost a son in Iraq? That's one reason he goes down there and tries to help. I know he's given some of them rides to the VA hospital."

"That's really nice of him. I guess I came across as pretty uncaring the other day. Maybe I just hadn't given it enough thought," Lucas said, and Maria could feel the invisible wall crumbling.

"It's a complicated situation. They're not all able to be reached. Some of them really are messed up—drugs and mental issues. So I can see your point too."

The lights blinked on and off a couple of times as if to tease them, but then they flickered one more time and stayed on.

So much had happened in a short time. They'd laughed about his wet clothes and her robe. She'd cried. They'd laughed some more. And he'd kissed her. Sort of. It had been soft and subtle, but it was a kiss nevertheless.

She hadn't forgotten how she'd been upset with him after he'd expressed his distaste for homeless people, but that was tempered now with his gentleness when she needed reassuring. His protection when she needed shelter. His concession of making a snap judgment. Lucas had brought calm to chaos, and in her opinion there had been a noticeable change in their relationship. They'd taken it to a new level, and she liked it.

"I guess our candlelight picnic is over," Lucas said as he stood up after blowing out the votives. "Kind of sad because I really enjoyed it, but I need to get back to Dallas anyway. Early day at the office tomorrow. Let me take these dishes back to the kitchen."

"I'll check your clothes in the dryer."

"Actually…if they're still wet, turn the dryer back on for a few minutes if you don't mind. There's something I want to ask you before I head home."

Chapter Twenty-Three

Sunlight filtered through the blinds on the west window of Lucas's office Thursday afternoon as he sat, wondering why in the world some guy named Max Kincade wanted to find Carmen. And even more surprising was the fact that Max had said he'd know Lucas when he saw him.

Cooper's voice cut into his thoughts. "I thought you were leaving early today."

"I am. As soon as I finish typing up this video deposition. Almost done."

"Let me know how the meeting with this Max fellow goes. That is really strange."

"Yeah. Weird, huh?"

As soon as Cooper left, Lucas drew in a long, slow breath and released it, sat up straighter in his chair, and let his fingers fly over the keys on his laptop. The sooner he could finish here, the sooner he could get on the road to Mauricio's Restaurant and hopefully solve the mystery surrounding Max Kincade. His reading taste ran to detective and spy novels, but he was even more intrigued when the plot involved his own life.

Within five minutes he'd finished for the day and emailed his work to himself, put it on a flash drive, and printed it. If law school had taught him anything at all, it was to be diligent in securing evidence.

While he was a little uneasy about the impending meeting with mystery man, he felt relief and happiness from the evening before with Maria. The weather had been a special blessing for two reasons. Since Maria was uneasy in storms, Lucas became the protector, a role he was quite happy to play. And the power outage had afforded them the opportunity to eat a romantic, if not unusual, dinner by candlelight.

Their time together had also given her the opportunity to talk about her weekend in Dallas with the church group, and Lucas had a keener understanding of her feelings about helping the homeless. He wasn't completely there yet, but at least her stories had given him something to consider.

But now he was on the highway en route to a meeting the outcome of which he couldn't begin to predict. Was this Max Kincade friend or foe or just some Joe Shmoe who actually *had* dated Carmen? He would know soon enough, he thought, as he steered his Toyota into the restaurant's parking lot.

He walked up to the hostess station at Mauricio's five minutes early, and because he didn't expect Max to be there, said to the hostess, "I'm meeting someone in a few minutes. I'll wait over here." He pointed to a bench.

"I believe your party is already seated. I'll show you to the table."

Already here? He hadn't expected that. In fact, he'd hoped to have a few minutes to prepare himself for the meeting. The same reason he always liked to get to court early: mental preparation. You never knew which way a judge or jury would rule, and it helped to be ready to deal with any possible outcome. In this case, he was completely in the dark and would have appreciated a few minutes to sit on the bench and contemplate. But it wasn't to be, so he followed the hostess as she maneuvered through the restaurant to a booth in the back where sat a man he was sure he'd never laid eyes on before. Fiftyish, he thought. Thinning hair. Average height and weight. Nothing unusual about his features.

The man stood as he walked up and extended his hand. "Max McBride, Mr. Avila. Explanation about the name later. Thanks for making yourself available on short notice."

"So you represented yourself as Max Kincade to my aunt, but that's not your name? How do I know whether to believe you now?"

Max reached into his pocket, took out his wallet, removed his driver's license, and handed it to Lucas.

"So why—"

"Have a seat and I'll explain everything. Do you mind if we order first? I'm starving. Do you like fajitas?"

"Yes, but—"

"I have an expense account and I never use it up completely, so…"

By that time a server had come to their table and asked about drinks. "We're ready to order. Fajitas for four, chicken and beef, with all the trimmings. And I'll have a margarita. Lucas?"

"No, thanks. Water for me," Lucas said. "That's a lot of fajitas." He hoped no one else was joining them. This whole situation was weird enough already.

"We can take home anything that's left over. Mauricio's fajitas are as good warmed up at home as they are here."

"Mr. McBride—"

"Max."

"Okay, but I'd like to know why you went to my aunt's house, introduced yourself as Max Kincade, lied about why you wanted to find Carmen. This is strange, to say the least."

"You got that right. It *is* strange. Probably the strangest thing Mr. B has asked me to do in the twenty years I've been on retainer with him. I'm a private detective, Lucas, and I've been tasked with finding your mother."

"Thomas Bennington. I suspected as much. But why does *he* want to find Carmen? And does he know you're telling me this?"

"He does. I ran it by him, and we both think it's time to take action and put some of the secrecy aside that's surrounded Everett Bennington for so long…and why he left home with little to no explanation. Of course, the boss didn't know about you until a few weeks ago, but the fact that Everett has a son changes everything, at least as far as your grandfather is concerned."

"But how do you know my aunt?"

"Mr. B saw the name Carmen Avila on your birth certificate, and I'm a private detective, so…"

"So you thought her sister might know where she is."

"She's a piece of work, that one!" He laughed. "Did you know she pulled a gun on me?"

"Well, that's Isabel for you. *Unpredictable* is her middle name."

"Do you think she knows where your mother is?"

"I've suspected it. But she won't tell me."

The server brought the sizzling fajitas to the table, and Max and Lucas started filling flour tortillas.

"I think we should join forces," Max said after a few bites. "I might know a way to get to that aunt of yours."

"I doubt it. She's a force to be reckoned with."

"I find that attractive in a woman, don't you?" Max took a sip of his drink and licked the salt off his lips.

Lucas found it difficult to believe that anyone would think that way about his aunt. "We've never been close. I don't think teaming up with me—to get information from her—would be your best bet."

"Hear me out. Did you happen to see a red BMW convertible in the parking lot?"

"I parked by one. Sweet wheels. Why?"

"It's mine and your aunt took a liking to it. Thinks it sexy. That's what she said. She called it sexy." Max threw his head back and laughed heartily. "I offered to buy her a new gun to tell me where her sister is, but that didn't faze her. I got the feeling the car just might do the trick, though."

Lucas shot Max an incredulous look. Surely he wasn't... "You can't be thinking about giving her your car just to get information about my mother."

"Of course not. But I might take her for a ride in it every once in a while. That could work. Heck, I'd even let her drive. How do you think she'd like to tool around town in a sexy red convertible?"

"I don't know. She didn't sound very happy about your showing up at her place the other day. But, as I said, she's unpredictable." Lucas paused a moment to think through his options. "What do we have to lose? I can't probate the will until I find Carmen, which means Isabel can't get her inheritance. It's not much, but to her it probably would seem like a lot. Of course, we don't know for sure she would be able to give us any information, but I got the feeling she knows something. She said a couple of times that Carmen didn't want to be found."

"I'd say that's pretty telling. So...what do you say? Try the car bribe?"

"Why not?" Lucas was fresh out of options.

Chapter Twenty-Four

Max still found it difficult to believe he was looking forward to seeing that crazy woman again. The one who pulled a gun on him. The one who called his car sexy. Truth be told, he found *her* sexy. He didn't know what it was about her. Maybe her spunk. He'd always been attracted to women with spunk.

Maybe the fact that she could read the situation well enough to know not to believe him. He'd always been attracted to intelligent women who could see right through his bravado.

Maybe he just liked her dark-brown, almost-black hair that matched her dark-brown, almost-black eyes. Or the way her ponytail swished and bobbed when she jerked her head around to give him the brushoff. Well, whatever it was, he hoped to heck Thomas Bennington would give him the go-ahead to tell her the truth. And he was chomping at the bit to find out as he dialed his boss's number Friday morning.

"Mr. B, I need to talk to you. Can you meet me somewhere, or do you want me to come to your office?"

"You found her?"

"Not yet. I have a plan, though, and I need your okay."

"Lunch at Texas Prime. You can buy me a steak with some of that ridiculous money I pay you to frolic around and amuse yourself. It's a good thing you hit a homerun every once in a while."

"Batting a thousand for you, chief. At least I will be if you give me a go-ahead on my latest idea."

"We'll see. Eleven-thirty."

On the Saturday that Lucas and a couple of his high school friends were scheduled to clean out Kacie's barn for the party, he showered and dressed in what he considered his most stylish work clothes, new jeans and an untucked, short-sleeve plaid shirt. Since the night of the storm, his anticipation at the thought of seeing Maria again was palpable.

Thankful the storm had given them an opportunity to reconnect in a somewhat romantic atmosphere—she seemed to enjoy the wisp of a kiss as much as he did— he'd asked her out before he left and let it be known he considered it a serious date. They were going into Dallas for dinner and a live production of *Sound of Music* at the Dallas Theater Center. Since his and Cooper's boss had a daughter in the play, Coop would be there, too, with a date, and Lucas thought it would be a perfect opportunity for him and Maria to meet.

Knowing he'd be lifting hay bales while working in the barn, Lucas rummaged around in the garage until he located a pair of work gloves. He entered the ranch's address into GPS. Twenty minutes. Time to go. He was supposed to meet Johnny and Carlos at the barn at ten o'clock. They'd break for lunch at noon, and if they weren't finished, would come back. The cleanup had to be completed soon so Maria and Kacie could start decorating.

When Lucas arrived at the ranch, his friends were already there. He recognized their cars in front of one of the barns. He also noticed Maria's car parked in the circular drive in front of the sprawling, red brick, ranch-style house.

An older man—seventies would be Lucas's guess—met him as he parked and got out of his car. Maria had told him Kacie's foreman would be supervising the cleanout but couldn't do much of the heavy lifting himself.

"Stewart Ross," the man said, extending his weathered hand. "Maria told me what kind of car to look for. I'm Kacie's ranch hand, but these old bones aren't as able as they use to be, and arthritis is not a fella's friend." His grin accentuated the wrinkles on his thin face.

"Pleased to meet you. I'm Lucas Avila. Don't worry, sir. We'll do a good job if you'll just tell us where to put things."

"That I can do. I've been working this ranch for the Griffins since 1988. Know every square inch of it like the back of my hand. Knew your grandpa too. A fine man, Joe was. We used to play checkers in front of the general store on an occasional lazy afternoon while your grandmama was shopping. I 'spect you were off to get your education by then. He was real proud of you."

"Thank you for saying that, sir. They were the best."

Just then Johnny and Carlos ambled out of the barn. "We thought we heard voices out here," Johnny said. "You ready to get to work, Lucas? There's plenty to be done in there."

"I'm glad y'all are doing this for Miss Sherise," Stewart said. "She's a real important part of this community." He clapped his hands together. "Let's go. It's not every day I have three hale and hearty youngsters to boss around, and I'll be mighty glad to get that old barn cleaned out."

Kacie and Maria had been working for an hour in the kitchen, putting together centerpieces of silk flowers and crystal vases on loan from a home decorating store on the square. "You seem pretty chipper today," Kacie said. "Even at school the last couple of days. Did something happen with you and Lucas?"

"You could say that." Maria grinned, remembering she'd always been transparent to Kacie. "Actually, he came over Wednesday night."

Kacie held a peony in midair and turned toward her friend. "The night of the storm?"

"Yeah. The night we lost power and the tornado went over my house."

"How romantic! Scary, but romantic."

"You have no idea! We ate dinner by candlelight, sitting on the floor in my closet. You know how I get in storms. But this time…this time was different. We took our food and went in there when the tornado warning sounded. Then—in about five minutes—the lights went out." Maria smiled and cut her eyes over at her friend.

Kacie took the hint. "He kissed you, didn't he?"

"Sort of."

"'Sort of' counts. But what about—"

"We talked it out. He was great. Wanted to know all about my day downtown. Plus…he's probably right concerning some of the people who live on the street. I know I tend to see the world through rose-colored glasses."

Kacie laughed and continued her flower arranging. "I can't disagree with that."

"And one more thing," Maria added. "He asked me out on a date. A *real* date. Dinner and a musical in Dallas in two weeks."

Kacie reached over and hugged her friend. "And all it took was a dark and stormy night. Thank goodness for Texas weather. When am I going to meet this guy? You've met Charlie."

"I could hardly keep from meeting Charlie since he teaches with us." Maria laughed. "But you can meet Lucas whenever you're ready. I saw his car outside. He's working in the barn now with two of his friends from high school."

"Does he know about Peter?" Kacie asked.

"Peter? There's nothing to know about Peter."

"Nothing to know?"

"That's right. Because Peter's in the past, and that's where he's going to stay."

"Okay, but I think it would be better if Lucas heard about him from you rather than someone else. You're fooling yourself if you think people have forgotten about him."

Lucas set down the broom and pulled his vibrating phone out of his jeans pocket. Max McBride. "Guys, I need to take this. Won't be long."

"Yeah?" he answered when he was outside the barn.

"Got the okay to go ahead from your grandpa. And Lucas? I will need you to give her a head's up that I'm coming and ask her to hear me out. Otherwise...well...she and 'Mr. Smith and Mr. Wesson,' as she calls it, might not be so forgiving this time."

"I'll talk to her," Lucas said. "When are you thinking about going?"

"She works, I assume?"

"Yeah. I think her shift runs eight to four Monday through Friday."

"So any day after, say…six? The sooner the better. Try for Monday. I'll see if she wants to take a little ride. Maybe it'll whet her appetite."

"If you can find out Carmen's whereabouts, I'll owe you."

"No you won't," Max countered. "Your grandfather pays me handsomely. He's a good man, Lucas. A little rough around the edges at times, but a good man."

"I'll get back to you after I talk with Isabel. Gotta run now, but I wish you good luck in dealing with my aunt. I don't want to discourage you, but it'll be a miracle if she gives you any information."

Chapter Twenty-Five

Lucas had been back inside working with Johnny and Carlos a few minutes when Maria and Kacie entered with glasses full of sweet iced tea. "We thought you guys might like something to drink." Maria set the tray down on one of the hay bales, her gaze sweeping across the clean barn floor, her mind marveling at how much three guys had been able to get done in a couple of hours.

"You betcha!" Johnny and Carlos said in unison, as they each grabbed a glass and quickly downed their drinks.

"Kacie, I think you met Johnny and Carlos already this morning, but this is Lucas Avila...my across-the-street neighbor when we were kids and again now. At least on weekends."

"Great to meet you, Kacie." Lucas extended his hand.

"So you're the Lucas I've been hearing so much about," she said, smiling and nudging her friend.

"Uh oh." Lucas flashed that crooked grin at Maria, and he thought he saw a hint of a blush appear on her cheeks.

"All good, I assure you," Kacie said.

"Well, that's a relief." Lucas smiled and winked at Maria and turned back to Kacie. "Thanks for letting us use your barn for the party. It's perfect."

"My pleasure. Sherise deserves to be honored. I'm glad Maria thought of it."

Maria piped up quickly to give credit where it was due. "Having the party in a barn was Lucas's idea."

"I meant the idea for the party, but that too. I'm glad my barn and I can be a part of it. Hey! Y'all are doing a great job! This old barn hasn't looked this good in…well…in my lifetime. By the time I came along, my parents had built the new one and had kind of let this one get run down. Stewart and I didn't know what to do with it."

Stewart, who had been standing silently in the background, chimed in. "The way these guys have it looking, I'm thinking we could turn it into one of them fancy wedding venues that are all the rage now."

Everybody laughed. "That's not a bad idea, Stewart," Maria said, "but there's a lot involved with weddings and you wouldn't want to run into one of those bridezillas."

"Yep. Things have sure changed since my heyday. I always say, 'People should spend less time on the wedding and more time on the marriage.' But then I'm an old bachelor so what do I know?" he said with a twinkle in his eye.

"You know more than most people, Stew," Kacie said. "I don't know what I'd do without you. We'll go and let you guys finish. Thanks for coming out and doing this. This party's going to be epic!"

Lucas, Johnny, and Carlos worked fast and were finished by twelve-thirty. If Kacie and Maria needed anything else done, he could do it, Stewart said. The hard part, the heavy lifting and cleaning, had been completed.

Lucas was glad to be free because he had a mission to accomplish. He was hoping to persuade Isabel to see Max again by telling her the truth about who the detective was, what he was trying to do, and why. Then it would be up to Max to persuade her to give them any information she might have about her sister. And if Max wanted to dangle his red convertible as a carrot, well…that was up to him. He couldn't imagine for the life of him what the detective found attractive about his aunt, but to each his own.

When Lucas arrived at Isabel's apartment, he wheeled his car beside hers, got out, and took the stairs two at a time. She answered on the first knock.

"Good," Lucas said. "At least you didn't meet me with your gun in hand." He entered her studio apartment and looked around. He hadn't been here in a long time, but everything looked the same as it had the whole time she'd lived above her friend's garage. Around twenty years if his memory was correct. She'd wanted to get out and on her own as soon as possible after high school graduation and when she landed a job at a local factory. There she'd been, day after day, doing the same thing, he imagined, although she didn't talk about it. And day after day she would come home and look at these same four walls and the daybed, rocker/recliner, card table, and two folding chairs Mama Rosa and Papa Joe gave her when she left home. That was it. Those were her furnishings.

What a life, he thought. But she seemed content. At least she didn't have to mow a yard or pay for a plumber when the toilet wouldn't flush. She'd bought herself a small TV and went to the library regularly. There was always a stack of books by her chair, and the rifle had stood guard by her bed as long as he could remember.

"I looked out the window when I heard a car pull up to make sure it wasn't that Kincade guy, but if he ever comes back, you'd better believe Mr. Smith and Mr. Wesson will greet him."

"You need to be careful with that thing, Isabel."

"My gun...or that guy whose story was too ridiculous to be believed?"

"Your gun, of course, but that guy's name is Max."

"What about him? So I guess you called him."

"I did. And he wanted me to apologize for him—although he's planning to do it too—but he wanted me to break the ice by telling you the real reason he came to see you."

"I *knew* he was lying," she said. "I can spot 'em a mile away."

"He's a private detective, and he works for Thomas Bennington."

"Your newly acquired grandfather who's worth millions?" Isabel raised one eyebrow. "I did a little research of my own."

"Yep. That's the one. Mr. Bennington wants him to locate Carmen. He thinks it will help in finding my father, his son. Even if she doesn't know where he is now, maybe she can shed some light on the situation to help us find him. Where and how they met, the last time she saw him, if he mentioned any place he might have wanted to go."

"And this involves me *how?*" Isabel asked.

"Do you mind if I sit down?"

"Sure. I have a nice chair here with your name on it. Not fancy like you're used to, but it'll keep you off the floor." She patted the back of one of the folding chairs.

Lucas sat down, put his elbows on the card table, and overlapped his hands for a chin rest. "Remember when you said Carmen doesn't want to be found?"

"I did say that, didn't I? Hmm. I didn't mean to."

"But you did." He sat up straight and nodded. "And because of that, I know you have some information that would help us find her. You either know where she is or how to get in touch with her. Don't you?"

"Mr. Kincade offered to buy me a new gun. What are you offering?"

"Actually, his name's Max *McBride*. He didn't tell you his real name because when he was here before, he hadn't obtained permission from Mr. Bennington to contact you. He has now."

"Okay. Fine. I don't care what his name is. What are you offering?"

"I told you I'd buy your third of the house, but we need to probate first, and we need Carmen to do that. But Max has another offer you might like too. He asked me to let him present his idea to you. Will you see him again and hear him out? And then will you, out of the goodness of your heart—" Lucas rolled his eyes mentally and hoped he hadn't done it noticeably. "—tell us what you know about Carmen?" He rested his case. It was all he had. He hoped it would work.

"She won't be happy with me." Isabel got up and started pacing.

"She won't have to know the information came from you. We could think of another possible way a private detective could have obtained it. What if we promise to keep you completely out of it?"

"I'm kind of interested now in what this Max guy has to say. At least he has good taste in cars."

"Good. I'll tell him to call you and set up a time to come back out. Or would you rather meet him somewhere?"

"He can buy me some barbecue. I haven't been to Uncle Rio's in a while."

"Great. I really appreciate this, Isabel. And leave your gun at home. He's not a threat. I can promise you that."

"Just call me and tell me when to meet him."

"I will. And thanks again." He rose and started toward the door.

"But I'm not promising anything," she added as an afterthought.

"I understand." He had an urge to hug his aunt—for the first time in years—but he didn't want to do anything that might make her change her mind, and he didn't know how receptive she'd be to an act of affection from her nephew. The thought of a hug reminded him of Sherise. He stopped and turned back toward Isabel. "You're going to Sherise's party next Saturday, right? Did Maria call you?"

"Yeah. I'm going. Sherise is one of the few people I like in this town, and I could count 'em on one hand."

"Good. I'll see you there."

Whew! That was easier than I expected, he thought after he got in his car, closed his eyes, leaned his head back, took a long breath, let it out slowly. *Maybe, just maybe, this is the beginning of finding out where I came from.*

Chapter Twenty-Six

Max McBride had called Isabel as soon as he'd heard from Lucas that she was willing to see him—on the condition he'd take her out for barbecue. Assuming she'd get a kick out of riding to the restaurant in his sexy—as she called it—red convertible, he'd offered to pick her up at six o'clock Monday evening, and she'd accepted.

When he arrived at her apartment, she was waiting for him on the landing. He was glad he was sitting down when he looked up and saw her. She wore a white sundress that accentuated her dark skin and hair…and red cowboy boots. A combination he wouldn't have thought would go together. Yet, on her it worked well. And he was blown away by her beauty. Who would have guessed a gun-totin', jeans-wearin', free-spirited wildcat could clean up like that? She hardly looked like the same person he'd encountered a few days ago, and he hoped her attitude toward talking about Carmen had changed as much as her appearance.

"Well, if it isn't Mr...er...Kincade? McBride? What should I call you?" She flipped her ponytail around the way she had a few days ago.

I see not everything's changed, he thought, thankful the spunk was still there. "I deserved that, but Max will be fine," he said as he started up the stairs, all of a sudden very aware of and bothered by his thinning hair.

"Don't come up. I know the way down."

He stopped, turned in his tracks, and went around to open the car door for her.

"So I'm getting treated to barbecue and a ride in your convertible because you think I have some info on my sister? Well...one reason is as good as another, I guess. I could lead you on like this for days, weeks, maybe even months."

Was she kidding, he wondered. She didn't seem to be, but he couldn't read her. *Yet* anyway. He was going to have to remedy that. "So you think you have some kind of power over me, do you?"

"He, in this case *she*, who has the information has the power. Wouldn't you agree?"

"To an extent. However, I'm not doing this for myself. I'm doing this for my boss and for your nephew, both of whom want to find your sister, but if, at any time, I get tired of bowing to your whims, I'm out. Plain and simple. No skin off my nose." *Two can play at this little game, missy. Don't you get too uppity...no matter how good you look tonight.*

They rode in silence for the next five minutes, the length of time it took them to get to the restaurant. He parked and rushed around to open the door for her. Might as well do everything he could to butter her up. It could be fun to string it out, but he didn't think his boss would play along forever. And Lucas *certainly* wouldn't understand. A thought that almost caused him to laugh out loud.

Max could have summed up the atmosphere in Uncle Rio's with one word: chaotic. He thought it unusually crowded and noisy for a Monday evening, but maybe that meant the food was unusually good too. He hoped so. The smell of mesquite-smoked meat had whetted his appetite, and he was all of a sudden ravenous.

Since they chose not to go through the buffet line, the hostess seated them in one of the few empty booths and took their drink orders. "I've never been here. What do you recommend?" he asked Isabel.

"I'm getting my usual, a brisket plate with creamed corn and fried okra. Do you want to look at a menu, though?"

"No. That sounds good. I'll go with that too."

Someone had apparently dropped a few quarters in the jukebox, because the sounds of "Boot Scootin' Boogie" floated throughout the room. People popped up from where they were sitting, pushed some tables away from the center of the room, and got in formation to line dance.

"Let's dance!" Isabel said.

"What? Are you kidding? I don't know how to do that."

"You live in Texas, and you don't know how to line dance? You can't be serious."

"As a heart attack. Which I might have if I were to try it."

"Come on," she insisted, grabbing his hand. "Just watch me and do what I do. And remember who has the power right now."

"Oh, for goodness' sake," he grumbled as he followed her to the improvised dance floor. What had he gotten himself into? Whatever it was, it had better pay off.

"So…" Isabel said when they were back at their booth after the song was over, "you wanted to come clean with me? I think that's what Lucas said. Just know this. I don't cotton to liars."

"Let me catch my breath, Miss Isabel. You have to remember I'm not used to this like you apparently are." Max took a long drink of water and some deep breaths. As much to figure out just what to say as anything else. He hadn't thought this out completely, but had decided to ad lib. Truth be told, he wasn't exactly sure how to get in—and stay in—her good graces. She had an exciting but volatile personality, and he didn't know what would set her off.

"You should get more exercise," she advised.

He was still somewhat out of breath, and his words came out slowly. "You're right about that. I should."

"Dancing is good exercise."

"You're right about that, too, but I don't want to die of a heart attack before I get in shape."

"If you don't get in shape, you probably *will* die of a heart attack," she shot back.

"You're not one to mince words, are you?"

"Never could figure out why I should."

"I thought about joining a gym once. Thought about it for…oh…maybe five minutes."

"Why would you do a stupid thing like that when you can get free exercise? I just don't understand some people. I don't understand *most* people, actually. I guess that's why I don't have any real friends."

"I don't believe that."

"You don't believe what?"

"That you don't have any friends. A dancing fool like you?"

Isabel slowly shook her head. "No. I really don't. Carmen always had a lot of friends. People flocked to her like moths to a flame. Me? Not so much. But it was okay. I couldn't tolerate most of the people at my school anyway. And don't even get me started on the people where I work."

The mention of Carmen sparked Max's memory of why he and Isabel were at Uncle Rio's together in the first place. "Since you brought her up... Carmen, I mean. I guess this would be a good time for me to offer an apology for trying to sell you a made-up story about why I wanted to find your sister."

"I'm all ears."

"I'm sorry I wasn't forthright with you about the reason I wanted to locate Carmen, but I was trying to leave my boss out of it. This whole situation with his son's disappearance has been hard on him and continues to haunt him after all these years. So when he met Lucas, well...that just brought up all the pain he had tried to put behind him. But he feels now that if he can talk with Lucas's mother, maybe some information she could give him...maybe it could shed some light on why Everett left home so many years ago. But anyway, I shouldn't have approached you the way I did. Just coming to your place without so much as a phone call. I hope you'll accept my apology."

"Depends."

"On what?"

"What's for dessert?"

Oh, my gosh! She put me through that whole spiel and all she wanted was a piece of chocolate cake! Max McBride had finally met his match.

Chapter Twenty-Seven

"If I give you information on how to find Carmen, will you let me drive your car back to my apartment?" Isabel asked after they'd finished dessert.

Max knew it wasn't going to be easy to get information out of Isabel, but letting her drive his car didn't seem like too much of a price to pay.

"I don't know," he replied. "Are you a safe driver?"

"You're a private detective. Check my record."

"I'll take your word for it. After all, someone who has such animosity toward liars—of which I am chief—wouldn't lie just to get to drive a sexy, red convertible. Would she?"

"She would not."

"Okay. You can drive her home. What info do you have for me?"

"I want your word…for what that's worth," she said laughing, "that you will make sure Carmen doesn't know I was involved in this at all."

"You have my word." She started to protest, and he put his hand up, palm toward her. "I didn't say that last time."

"Fair enough," Isabel said. "Okay. I assume you've been looking for Carmen Avila."

Max nodded.

"She hasn't gone by that name for years. About fifteen, I imagine."

"I hope you have more for me. That hunk of cheesecake you had for dessert cost $5.99," he said.

"Wilson."

"She's married?"

"Divorced. But she kept the name, for some reason I'll never be able to fathom. I guess she didn't think Avila sounded like a proper name for a highfalutin business woman."

"I'm gonna need more. Husband's first name? There will be a record of the marriage and the divorce. Maybe now we're getting somewhere."

"I can do better than that."

"Great. Shoot." Max thought about his word choice, sat up straight, and shook his head vigorously. "Didn't mean that literally."

"I haven't driven Ruby yet."

"You named my *car*?"

"Yep. Let's go. Or I could play 'Achy Breaky Heart' on the juke, and we could dance again. Your call."

He tossed her the key. "You drive a hard bargain."

"Come into my humble abode. Emphasis on humble," Isabel said when they arrived at her apartment after she had cruised around Trinity Springs in Ruby for about fifteen minutes. That's all the time it took to go up and down the major streets in town.

"It seems you have the necessities," Max said as they entered and he looked around.

"Suits me. But you didn't come in to write a review of my digs, did you?"

"Indeed, I didn't. What do you have for me?"

"Again, you did *not* get this information from me."

"You have my word…which you should know by now is worth something…since you just drove Ruby home."

"She owns a cleaning business. It's pretty big now. Houses and offices. I think she has about fifty employees."

"In Dallas?"

"Yep."

"Name?"

"Bizzy Bee Cleaning Services."

"Thank you! That's a *huge* help. Do you want to take Ruby for another spin around town next week?"

"No. I'm one and done. I guess Lucas deserves to know his mother…now that Mama's gone."

"Why, Miss Isabel! Is that a soft spot I detect?"

"No. It's not. Now get on out of here before I change my mind about Ruby."

"If you change your mind, you have my number." As an afterthought he said, "I do have one more question…if you don't mind answering it."

"Maybe. Maybe not."

"How do you know all this about Carmen?"

Isabel heaved a heavy sigh. "You might as well sit down." She motioned him to one of the folding chairs at the card table and he took a seat. "I'm the only one in the family who knew where she was. She contacted me after her divorce. Wanted to keep in touch to hear how Lucas was doing from time to time but didn't want Mama and Papa to know where she was or what she was doing. I think she felt guilty for deserting her son like she did and for putting the burden on them but didn't think it would be a good idea to come back into his life. She was satisfied to know he was okay. I mean he was better than okay really. When he came to live with us, he got all the attention. It was as if I'd moved out of the house already, but I didn't do that for another five years. Got out as soon as I could support myself." She paused and rolled her eyes. "Oh my goodness. I don't know why I'm telling you all this. Barbecue, cheesecake, and a red convertible have turned me into a blabbermouth."

"It was probably the dancing, but I'm glad you felt like you could tell me."

"Get on out of here before I say too much."

Max couldn't believe his luck. He hadn't expected to get that much information out of Isabel. The name of Carmen's business, for goodness' sake. That was all he needed. Mr. B would be impressed. Max didn't know what his boss was expecting, but surely not this. Not something that would lead them directly to Lucas's mother. The next step would be up to Thomas Bennington, and Max couldn't wait to find out what that would be.

Chapter Twenty-Eight

The rest of the week crept at a snail's pace for Lucas as he deposed witness after witness for a trial that was set to start on Monday of the next week. But during the depositions, all he could think about was Maria. Looking back to their stormy night and forward to their date kept him from getting bored with dry testimony of people who had been treated unfairly—or so they alleged—by the large corporation the opposing law firm represented. There were times when he wondered, though. About whether he was on the right side of the lawsuit in cases like this. And sometimes it unnerved him to the point of rethinking his career.

But Friday afternoon finally arrived and with it the anticipation of seeing Maria again and surprising Sherise with a birthday party on Saturday. Maria had asked him to say a few words, and talking about his mentor and the impact she'd had on him was the easiest speech he'd ever written. His only problem was cutting it down from five minutes to two or three. Other people would be speaking too, so he couldn't hog the stage, but there was no end to the imprint she'd made on his life. How did one pay proper tribute to a Sherise Washington in only a few minutes? Nevertheless, he'd cut it a bit and texted the band to play a special song at the end. He would ask Sherise to dance, and he knew she'd willingly oblige. She loved music and dancing almost as much as she loved investing in people.

He left the office an hour early in hopes of beating the traffic on the tollway, but in Dallas there was no such thing as beating Friday afternoon traffic. It started right after lunch and ended sometime in the wee hours of Saturday morning. Lucas didn't mind taking it slow and easy, though, once he got out of the city. He could ease back on the gas pedal, breathe in fresh country air, and delight in mile after mile of freshly plowed fields that awaited spring planting.

Growing up in a small, rural town an hour away from the city, he'd taken for granted many things: the beauty of the land, the peace and quiet of the neighborhoods, the genuine friendliness of the townspeople. He'd been away for nine years, since he'd started college, but coming back after Mama Rosa's passing had reignited something in him. Call it a yearning for home...or getting back to his roots. No. Not roots. Because he didn't know much about his roots. But that's what he intended to remedy. And he now had the resources of an actual private detective to help him with that.

Lucas was antsy to find out if Max had been able to get any information from Isabel, but there was nothing he could do but wait to hear from the detective or his grandfather. What was the protocol for finding one's birth parents after a lifetime of knowing nothing? He wasn't sure how this would go, but he was trying to stay positive.

As if on cue, his phone rang when he was about five minutes from his destination. A quick glance told him it was Thomas Bennington.

"Son, I have an encouraging bit of news for you."

"Yes, sir?"

"It seems your birth mother has been located, thanks in part to your aunt and my detective. I believe you've met Max."

"Yes, I have." Lucas's posture stiffened in the driver's seat, and he cleared his throat. "By...by 'located' do you mean you know her exact whereabouts? And have you spoken with her?"

"We know where to find her, but we haven't contacted her. I'm going to leave that up to you and ask you to report back to me after you've talked with her. Max will get you the contact information. And Lucas?"

"Yes, sir?" His hands tightened on the wheel.

"It was my choice to let you speak with your mother first, but keep in mind that I have a stake in this too. I'm interested in finding out why Everett chose to leave home and if there's a possibility of his coming back. Of course, she might not be able to shed any light whatsoever on those questions. But it's worth a try. I know you need to notify her of the passing of your grandmother in order to probate the will. But I'm hoping you can get some information from her as well."

"I'll do the best I can, sir. I know it means a lot to you too."

A few minutes after they'd hung up, Lucas was sitting in his car in the driveway of his house on Bailey Street with a kaleidoscope of emotions—relief, anticipation, fear—when Maria tapped softly on his window and he jumped. He lowered the window.

"I didn't mean to startle you." She laughed. "I saw you pull up and thought I'd say hi."

"Sorry. I was deep in thought. But I'm glad it's you."

"I'm glad you're glad." Her voice was soft, and it served to calm Lucas a little.

"Let's go in," he said. "I have something to tell you." It was time. Their relationship was at a stage where he felt comfortable sharing with her the discovery of his father's name and his mother's location.

Lucas laid it all out on the table, starting with finding his birth certificate. He told her about talking with Thomas Bennington, Sr. and taking a DNA test. About trying to get information from Isabel. About meeting Max. All the way to the phone conversation he'd just had with his grandfather.

Maria was spellbound. This was something so intimate that she was surprised but pleased Lucas chose to tell her everything. "You've kept this all bottled up inside this whole time? Dealing with it by yourself?"

"Sherise and my friend Cooper know a little, but they don't know Carmen has been located. I'll never be able to figure out how Max got that information out of Isabel."

"Thank you for telling me this. I can imagine how much it means to you to be able to talk to your mother and potentially find your father. Bennington. I wonder if my parents know—"

"I'm not ready for anyone else…well, you know."

"Of course. I understand. I won't say anything."

"It's a relief just being able to tell you about it. You don't know how many times I've wanted to."

Maria was happy to be a sounding board for Lucas, a safety net to catch him when he needed a safe place to land. "I'm really glad you did."

"Abrupt change of subject," he said, "but do we need to do anything tonight for the party?"

"I don't think so. Kacie and I will put the finishing touches on the barn tomorrow. Mama has the food deliveries all lined up. You might want to touch base with the band tonight to be sure they know what time to arrive and where to park."

"Can do. Want to get a bite to eat? Or have you already eaten?"

"No. I was hoping you would be here early and want to go somewhere."

"Or we could order pizza," Lucas said. "I'll be okay tomorrow, but I don't feel like being around a bunch of people tonight."

"Sure. But no pineapple. That's a deal breaker."

"Mushrooms and black olives?"

"Yes!"

Maria and Lucas spent the rest of the evening eating pizza and talking…about the party, his newly discovered grandfather, their jobs. He held her hand as he walked her back across the street in the moonlight. When they got to her door, he brushed a lock of hair off her face with his hand, pulled her close, and kissed her. This time it wasn't a "sort of" kiss. This time Maria knew it wasn't an accidental brushing of their lips together as her knees became weak and she leaned into him.

"Save me a dance tomorrow?" he said without letting go.

"Your name dominates my dance card, sir," she assured him as she laid her head against his chest.

He hugged her a little more tightly. "I guess I'd better let you go in, huh?"

"Unless you want me to fall asleep standing here like this."

"Don't tempt me," he whispered as he kissed her forehead and opened the door for her. "See you tomorrow."

Chapter Twenty-Nine

Paul Carpenter had been turning over an idea in his head for a couple of months, but he would need to coordinate with some other people before acting on it. Before even mentioning it to a few of the veterans on the street. On Saturday morning, he took his cell out of his pocket and dialed Rob Vargas's number. He wasn't surprised to find him working in his yard. Rob had often volunteered to help with landscape maintenance at the church, even though he lived thirty minutes away and rarely attended Sunday services. Paul suspected Maria put him up to it.

"If you have a minute," Paul said, "I'd like to run an idea by you. Be honest, though, if you don't think it will work. I can always revert to Plan B, so don't feel obligated."

"Sure. What do you have on your mind, Pastor?"

"You know those guys I work with in Dallas? Many of them are veterans."

"Yeah. Maria told us a little bit about your work."

"Well, I was wondering—and I'm just spitballing here—but I was wondering how you would feel about taking one or two of them fishing if I brought them out to your place. I think it would do them a world of good to get away from all that concrete. Some of them haven't been out of downtown Dallas in years."

"Oh my! That's terrible," Rob said, remembering how happy he was to get out of the city. "Always glad to introduce the lake to new people. I don't imagine they could get away from here without sitting down to a Livvy Vargas meal, though. Would that be a problem?"

"Problem? I'm sure they would consider a home-cooked meal quite a treat," Paul said. "I'm thinking about starting with a couple of guys who were in Desert Storm. Both around your age, I suspect, and one is kind of quiet, while the other one talks enough for both of them. They usually stick together on the street. I think Shane could talk Benny into it."

"You're talking about a weekend, I guess."

"Yeah. Let me run it by them and see if they'd be interested. I wanted to talk with you first. Thanks for being open to the idea. This could mean so much to some of these guys. I'll be in touch."

After Paul had hung up, he sat pondering whether he'd have time to run down to Dallas and present his idea to Benny and Shane and a few others or if he should wait. Thinking about what a day on the lake could mean to some of the veterans, he decided to make a quick trip into the city. He wasn't serving a meal this time, but he had a few cartons of protein bars in his car to hand out. Actually, he thought, that *would* be a meal for many of them.

When he reached the corner where he'd seen Shane and Benny last, they were nowhere to be found. Their gear was there, but it was being guarded by someone he'd seen only once or twice. The turnover rate had been high lately. He supposed it was due to the inflation that had hit people especially hard in recent months. Apartment rent had gone up, and that had caused many evictions.

"Hi, Willie," he said to the one in charge of protecting a couple of tents and some sleeping bags.

"How you know my name?"

"I met you last weekend. But I had some other people with me, so you might not remember."

"Oh, you with that church?" Willie asked.

"That's right. I'm looking for Shane and Benny. Do you know where they are?"

"At the liberry. Trusted me with their things. I'm new here, but they know a good man when they see one."

"I suspect that's right. And you seem to be taking good care of everything. I'm sure they appreciate it. Can you still keep an eye on things and help me pass out these protein bars?"

"Yes, sir! I can do that!" Willie seemed to be excited at the prospect of helping. Paul made a mental note: *Willie has a servant's heart.*

"Do you know what time the guys will be back, Willie?"

"I 'spect soon. They been gone what seems like a long time already."

"Would you like me to stand guard while you take a little break?" Paul offered.

"No, sir. I can't do that. They expect me to watch their stuff…and that's what I'm gonna do."

Paul smiled and made another mental note: *I'll bet Willie would enjoy some time on the lake too.*

Not long after all the protein bars had been handed out, Paul spotted Shane and Benny coming down the street, each with a book in his hand. That was strange, he thought. Was the library allowing them to check out books now? He walked up and met them halfway."

"Hi, guys."

Shane spoke up. "Look, Paul. Benny's friend Hannah checked out these books for us in her name and let us take them out of the library."

"She's your friend too," Benny said.

"She likes you better."

"Only 'cause she knows me better."

"Paul," Shane continued, "did you know the library has comic books? That's what I got. Benny got something a little more educational."

"Yeah? That was nice of her, huh?" Paul said.

"I think she has a crush on my boy Benny here." Shane punched his friend in the arm.

"We gotta go relieve Willie. He'll be wanting to find some lunch."

"He's eating a protein bar. Saved a couple for you guys too." Paul reached in his pocket. "Here ya go."

"Thanks, man!" Shane said.

"Yup." Benny nodded.

"I wanted to run something by you guys. I have a friend who lives on a lake and likes to take people fishing. How would you like to go fishing one day out at Cypress Grove?"

"You're kidding, right?" Shane's eyes widened.

"Nope. I'm dead serious."

"Paul wouldn't say something like that if he didn't mean it," Benny reminded him.

"I ain't been fishing since I was a kid and went with my grandpa. Benny, what about you?"

"Never."

"What?"

"Never been fishing."

"So what do you think?" Paul asked. "Would you like to go sometime?"

"Sure!" Shane pumped his fist in the air. "Benny?"

"Why?"

"Why what?" Paul put a hand on Benny's shoulder.

"Why does he want to take us fishing?"

"He just enjoys it and likes to see other people have fun catching fish. He lives on the lake and has a nice boat, so it's something he can do. You know how those people from the church come down here and bring food? Well, he doesn't do that, and this is his way of paying back people who risked their lives to fight for our freedom. People like the two of you."

"Anybody else going?" Shane said. "Or just us?"

"Just the two of you for now. I'll see if others want to go later."

"Can Willie go?" Benny asked.

"He can be in the second group in a few weeks. Rob's boat will hold three people comfortably but not four. Do you guys remember Maria who played her guitar and sang for us? Rob is her dad. Her parents live out at Cypress Grove Lake. It's about an hour north of here. I'd pick you guys up and bring you back. What do you say?"

"She played a song for me," Benny recalled.

"That's right. She did," Paul said. "And her parents are nice like that too."

"Let's go, Benny," Shane pleaded. "It's that guitar lady's parents. You liked her."

"We can't leave our stuff that long. And we can't ask Willie to watch it that long."

"We'll take it with us," Paul offered. "I'll help you pack it up."

"Why do you do this for us?" Benny asked.

"Why did you go to Kuwait and risk taking a bullet for me?"

"Fair enough." He looked down and seemed to be studying his shoes. "I'll go."

Chapter Thirty

Lucas had a lot on his mind early Saturday afternoon as he showered and dressed for Sherise's birthday party. He knew many guys would be there in jeans, but he thought this special occasion honoring a special lady called for a little more. Chinos and a navy polo seemed right, and he spent more time than usual taming his cowlick. After all, he'd be on stage, so to speak, for a few minutes and then on the dance floor with the honoree after that. He'd asked the band to invite everyone to join them on the dance floor after a minute or two.

But Sherise wasn't the only lady he was trying to impress. Since Wednesday night, Maria had been uppermost on his mind. He caught himself reliving the closet picnic when he was in his car, his office, his apartment. Even in court as he questioned witnesses, he would have to reel in his thoughts and get himself back on track. He was surprised she hadn't shown up in his dreams. She'd promised him some dances, and he couldn't wait to hold her in his arms again.

At two-thirty, Lucas eased into one of the many parking spaces behind the barn. Only a few other cars were there. He recognized pickups belonging to two of the band members: Toby, the bass player, and Derek, the steel guitar player. The other three would arrive shortly, they assured him as they carried their instruments into the barn to begin setting up in a corner.

When he entered the venue, he was amazed. A transformation had taken place since he'd last seen the space. Hundreds of tiny white lights were strung back and forth across the ceiling, and tables were adorned with bright tablecloths, food, and flowers. Hay bales lined the walls and folding chairs had been set up, but there was empty space in the middle of the floor for mingling and dancing. A huge, colorful HAPPY BIRTHDAY sign dominated the wall directly across from the entrance.

Clyde Gilmore had been the mayor of Trinity Springs for seven years and would likely win re-election when this term expired. Maria had asked him to emcee the event, so he was testing the speakers and mic. When he spotted Lucas, he motioned him to come over. "Son, why don't you test for volume since you'll be speaking. I'll say a few words of welcome and introduction, then Sherise's brother George, then Tina, then you. Maria tells me you want to be last because you have a special song the band is going to play at the end of your speech."

"George is here?" Lucas had, at one time or another, met all of Sherise's siblings.

"Yep. Came all the way from Chicago. Tina knew how to get in touch with him. Sherise has no idea George and his wife are in town."

Kacie walked up. "Mr. Mayor. Lucas. What do y'all think of the decorations?"

"Everything looks great, especially the lights. Did you do that?" Lucas asked.

Kacie took a bow. "Maria helped, of course."

Clyde chimed in. "Yep. You and Maria have done a fine job. Miss Sherise will be so pleased. Excuse me," he said, nodding to his wife across the way. "My better half is waving me over, and when Mama says 'jump,' Papa says 'how high.' Y'all just *think* I'm the mayor." He reared his head back and laughed heartily, causing his oversized belly to jiggle.

"I'm glad Maria asked him to emcee," Lucas said when Clyde was out of earshot. "He'll keep the party lively."

Kacie heard a ping and pulled her phone out of her jeans pocket. "That was Livvy asking if I could round up some guys to help Rob put ice and drinks in the tubs. Want to help? We have about twenty minutes to finish everything."

"Sure."

"Look for a maroon truck behind the barn."

For about fifteen minutes, Lucas and Rob worked filling up the tubs with drinks and ice while Livvy and Kacie fussed over the food and flowers and balloons.

All of a sudden, Clyde whistled through his teeth and grabbed the mic. "Y'all get quiet. They just rounded the corner into the driveway and should be walking in soon. Be ready to yell 'Surprise!' and then the Red Hill Boys will play 'Happy Birthday' and we'll all sing. Then I'll say a few words. Shhh! I hear them. Get ready."

After Sherise was inside and the singing had stopped, she slapped her hands to her cheeks. "Ooowee! I can't believe it! Y'all really surprised me!"

Maria found Lucas in the crowd. "She knew, didn't she?"

"I couldn't tell, but even if she did, she'll still enjoy the party."

Clyde picked up the mic again. "Y'all get quiet now. We're gonna eat and start the music in a minute, but I just wanted to say a couple of words. Miss Sherise, we're here to honor you today. Look at how many people came out to your birthday party. They all know... *We* all know that you're the heart of Trinity Springs. Heck, even your competitors are here and contributed food to this shindig. A couple of people are going to pay special tribute to you in a little while, but before we do that, let's eat—y'all form two lines to the right—and let's have some more music from the Red Hill Boys. Take it away, boys!"

"So far so good," Lucas said to Maria. "What a crowd! Looks like everybody we invited came...and then some. Let's get in line."

The temperature in the barn hovered just below ninety, but in spite of that Lucas could tell people were having fun. When he and Maria had filled their plates and picked up ice cold drinks from one of the tubs, they joined the Vargases outside under the shade of a live oak where they had set up four lawn chairs.

"Lucas," Rob said, "do you remember these chairs?"

"Not really. Should I?"

"These are the same chairs Joe and Rosa sat in while the four of us watched you and Maria run around catching fireflies and roller skating up and down the sidewalk many years ago. Those were the days. Good days."

"*Many* years ago? Daddy! Don't make me old before my time." She reached over and gave him a peck on the cheek.

"Well," he continued, "a lot has happened since then so it seems like a long time ago."

"Yes, sir," Lucas agreed. "In many ways it does, but something about today has kind of taken me back to those days. I get a little nostalgic when I come back to Trinity Springs. It was a good place to grow up."

"Sometimes I wish we hadn't moved Maria to Dallas, but at least she was smart enough to come back."

"And we were too," Livvy inserted.

"I guess I'm stuck in Dallas since that's where work is," Lucas said. "But as least I can come back on weekends. It's been good to get out of the city for some mini vacations recently."

Livvy touched his shoulder. "We hope you'll continue to come back often. I'm sure Rob would be glad to take you out on the lake again. And I'm always happy to put another plate on the table."

"Thank you. I appreciate that."

"I hate to cut this short," Maria interrupted, "but Clyde just texted me that it's time to start the tributes. Then some dancing and then you and I will sing, Daddy. You ready to talk, Lucas? Ready to sing, Daddy?"

"I'm ready," Rob said.

"What are y'all singing?" Lucas asked.

"I think we'll surprise you. What do you think, Daddy?"

"You'll like it, Lucas. I heard them practicing," Livvy inserted. "It's perfect for Sherise. Especially on her sixty-fifth birthday. In fact, I can't think of a song that's a better fit for her."

"Can't wait to hear it then." Lucas rose and took Maria's empty plate and drink can. "Guess I'd better get in the queue for the tributes."

In a couple of minutes Clyde blew into the microphone and tapped it a few times. "Is this thing on? Can y'all hear me?"

Shouts of "Loud and clear" and "We can hear ya, Clyde!" got his attention, and he spoke. "Miss Sherise, I know you were especially surprised to see your brother here for this celebration, and he has asked to say a few words. After that, a couple of other people will be speaking. So George, all the way from the big city of Chicago, come on up."

George made his way through the crowd and took the mic. "I love you, sis!" He blew her a kiss. "And apparently I'm not the only one, from the looks of this crowd. I'm sure most of you here know my story, but I'm gonna tell it anyway. I'll make it brief. Sherise was eight years old when I was born. She had lost her mother when she was five, and our dad married my mother a year later. I was the first offspring of that marriage, and my twin sisters came along two years after me. Our mother died giving birth to them. Our dad spiraled down into depression and was never the same, but Sherise took over and became our mom. If she hadn't been there for us, I don't know what would have happened. I do know that I wouldn't be a stockbroker in Chicago now. It started with all those multiplication tables you made me memorize, Sis. That began my love of numbers and math. Anyway, I speak for my sisters who couldn't be here, Sherise—and for myself—when I say we love you so much and wish you a very happy birthday and many more." He handed Clyde the mic and went over and put his big arms around Sherise, who was wiping tears off her cheeks.

The mayor stepped to the right and passed the microphone to Tina.

"I'm kinda nervous so bear with me. I ain't used one of these things before." She pointed to the microphone, and laughter from the audience helped her relax. She took a deep breath and continued. "All y'all know I been working for Sherise Washington a long time. But what you might not know is that about twenty-five years ago, when I was a single mom with three kids and had never had a real job, she took a big chance on me. She even let me bring my kids to the café sometimes when they weren't in school or I couldn't afford a babysitter. She would set them down at a table with coloring books or library books while I waited tables. Two of those kids are here today to help celebrate the lady they call their adopted grandma. Wave your hands out there, Emily and Adam. Anna lives too far away and couldn't make it, but she wanted me to tell Miss Sherise and all of y'all that she's a teacher now because of the love she got in the café. So, Sherise, you know I'd walk over hot coals for you. Happy birthday, my friend!"

Applause broke out, along with shouts of "We love you, Tina!" and "You done good!"

Lucas stepped up, and she handed him the mic. "George and Tina are hard acts to follow, but I'll try to put into words what this special lady has meant to me over the years. George, I know what you mean about multiplication tables, along with state capitals and sentence diagramming. She even made me memorize the preamble to the Constitution. All of these things have been important parts of my life and no doubt contributed to my chosen career. However, none were as important as the fact that she was always there for me. There to listen. There to give good advice. There to instill in me the confidence that I could do anything I set my mind to. But it's not all about me. And I'm sure George and Tina—and probably all of you—would agree with me on this. It's about community. I'll bet there's not a person here who hasn't been greeted with a hug and an encouraging word from Sherise when you've walked into the café or met her on the street. I'll bet she remembers the names of your children and grandchildren too. And asks to see current pictures of them when you come into the café. When she's talking to you, you feel like you're her best friend, don't you? The truth is…we all are. I grew up thinking I was her favorite person, her best friend. But it hit me one day that I'm not." He pointed to people in the audience. "You are. And you are. And you are. Sherise, I want you to know that while I realize that you're an equal opportunity friend to all of us, you'll always be my girl. May I have this dance?"

On that cue, the band started playing "My Girl," and Lucas strolled over and held out his hand to his mentor. She wiped some more tears, reached up, kissed his cheek, and whispered in his ear, "But you really *are* my favorite."

They occupied the dance floor alone for about a minute, when someone from the band said, "Lucas and Sherise would like to invite everyone else to join them."

As soon as their dance was over, people gathered around Sherise to offer their own words of appreciation, and Isabel sauntered over to Lucas and narrowed her eyes. "I guess you know I met with that Max guy...but if she ever finds out..."

"Carmen? She won't," he said. "Max and I agree on that. I'm going to talk to her Monday, and if she wants to know how I found out, I'll tell her I hired a really good private detective so we could probate the will. As far as you know, she doesn't know about Mama Rosa's death, does she?"

"I wouldn't know. I haven't heard from her in a long time."

Maria wandered over. "It's good to see you again, Isabel."

"Hi, Maria. You grew up real pretty. I knew you would," Isabel said.

"She did, didn't she? I was just about to ask her to dance. Excuse us, Isabel." Lucas took Maria's hand and whirled her onto the dance floor.

"Was that kind of abrupt?" Maria asked.

"With Isabel? We were finished," he said. "Plus. I'd really rather dance with you than talk to her. You don't mind, do you?"

"No. I just didn't want to hurt her feelings."

"Don't worry. Isabel and I are okay, but you're tenderhearted and concerned with other people's feelings. I love that about you."

She laid her head on his shoulder and he nuzzled her hair, recalling that same scent of flowers from their evening in the closet.

After several more minutes of Texas Two-Stepping and line dancing, Clyde called on Maria and Rob for a song. Maria took the mic. "Sherise, Dad and I thought this was the perfect song for you today, so we want to do it as a duet. We know you love George Jones, and this is one of his. It's called "I Don't Need Your Rocking Chair." Maria played her Martin, and Rob rocked out with his fiddle for about three minutes as some people in the audience danced and others just tapped their feet in rhythm. Sherise smiled from ear to ear, clapped her hands, and bobbed her head to the music.

No. She wasn't about to need a rocking chair *any* time soon.

Chapter Thirty-One

When Lucas rolled over and rubbed his eyes early Sunday morning, his first thought was of Maria. The nearness of her when they were dancing. Her smile that encouraged him when he was speaking about Sherise. The anticipation of taking her on their first real date next weekend.

He let himself daydream for a while before snapping to attention and refocusing his mind on another matter. The information Max had obtained from Isabel and Thomas had given to him. And suddenly his thoughts were not so pleasant. It was information he'd wanted, but now he didn't know exactly how to handle it. Should he go to see her in person? Send a letter? Make a phone call?

Showing up unannounced at Thomas Bennington's office had worked out well for him, but for some reason he didn't have that kind of resolve when it came to his mother. He'd had a hard time even referring to her as his mother and opted to think of her merely as Carmen Avila instead. Carmen Wilson now. He felt no personal affection for the woman who had given birth to him and then abandoned him. Wouldn't recognize her if he ran into her on the street. Didn't know how he would react when they met face to face.

On the other hand, he realized he would have to be the one to give her the news that her mother had passed away, and although she hadn't been involved in Mama Rosa's life for many years, she was still her mother. The woman who had raised her. Surely she would have some emotional response. Because of that, he thought it might be best to break the news over the phone. A letter was definitely too impersonal, and a visit might prove too awkward. Yes, a phone call first, and then—depending on how the conversation went—maybe a meeting later. He'd promised to try to get some information about Everett for Thomas, and he wanted that for himself too. He had so many questions, but they would have to wait. He wouldn't spring them on her at first.

Since Lucas had discovered the name of his father, he'd grown accustomed to grabbing a quick bite for lunch and eating in his car. Lunch hours were rarely about sitting down to a leisurely meal anymore. He was dealing with too many things and couldn't take any more time off work without a very good reason. So, not wanting to go into detail with his boss, he opted to conduct personal business on his own time.

Tomorrow he would make that phone call. But today he needed to be with Maria. She had a calming effect on him and would understand his uneasiness about talking with his mother. Knowing Maria would be at church until around noon, he decided to text her about the afternoon. Maybe a drive out to the lake. Or a picnic. Outdoors this time.

Coffee first, though, so he wouldn't text something undecipherable, he thought as he padded down the hall to the kitchen. After pouring himself a giant mug of caffeine, he picked up his phone.

Lucas: You busy this afternoon?
Maria: Not really. Why?
Lucas: I was thinking about taking a drive somewhere. Maybe a picnic. In good weather this time.
Maria: Sounds good. What time?
Lucas: I'll pick you up at 4:00. Will that work?
Maria: Sure. See you then!

In the early afternoon, around two o'clock, dark gray clouds formed in the western sky, and Lucas began to worry. The last storm was more of a blessing than a curse, but he'd been hoping for something different this time. He felt the need to be outdoors and wanted to ask Maria's opinion about how he was planning to approach Carmen. Since there was nothing he could do to change the weather, he busied himself with more cleaning, sorting, and packing in the garage—in an effort to make the time pass faster.

As he was putting some of Papa Joe's power tools in a box, a thought crossed his mind. *I wonder if Rob could use these? After all, they worked on projects together several years ago.* He decided to ask him before donating them. But not today. Today he wanted to be alone with Maria. A few weeks ago he had to stretch his brain to remember her, and now he couldn't get her out of his mind.

He worked for another hour before going in to shower. Lucas tried not to let himself dwell on the fact that his mother had abandoned him, preferring to think about the good life he had with Mama Rosa and Papa Joe. But sometimes the thought of Carmen's rejection reared its ugly head, and he had to use self-talk to get back to a happy place. He would picture himself the son of a woman who had to work all hours of the day and night just to keep a roof over their heads and food on the table. Then growing up in his grandparents' house didn't seem like the worst option.

The hardest part had been at school when kids would ask him why he lived with his grandparents, not his parents. Where was his mom? Who was his dad? And he'd have to say "I don't know" to all their questions. They eventually quit asking him, though, and accepted the fact that his life was a little different from the lives of most of his classmates.

By a quarter till four, the rain had stopped, and a double rainbow arched itself over the eastern sky. He was ready to pick up Maria but didn't want to rush her, so he decided to kill a few minutes by checking his phone for messages and email. Max had sent a text asking what he planned to do about the information Thomas had given him regarding his mother. He texted back that he was going to call her tomorrow and tell her about Mama Rosa's death. Then the ball would be in her court.

Max reminded him that Mr. B was hoping to get some information that would help him understand why Everett left home, and Lucas reminded Max that he was too. In fact, he wanted to know everything about the relationship of his biological parents. But he was going to have to play it by ear. A lot was riding on Carmen's reaction. He might have to take it slow and easy if she wasn't forthcoming with information. Be prudent with his cross-examining skills. Coming on too strong could cause her to clam up completely, and then they might never know.

"Where are we going?" Maria asked when Lucas showed up at her door.

"I thought we might pick up some sandwiches and drinks and go to the park. Unless you have a better idea."

"Not really. I'm just along for the ride. And the food. And, of course, the company."

"I'm glad you threw that in…even if it *was* as an afterthought."

"It was actually my first thought, but I didn't want to seem too forward." She winked.

Lucas grabbed her hand and headed down the sidewalk. "Come with me!" He led her out into the middle of the street.

"Look over there," he said, pointing to the eastern sky.

"A double rainbow! How beautiful."

He looked at Maria, pulled her close, and kissed her…right there in the middle of Bailey Street. "'Beautiful' is an understatement."

The rest of the afternoon and evening passed all too fast for Lucas, and before he knew it, they were packing up the quilt and picnic things. He needed to get back to Dallas at a reasonable hour because he had a big day ahead of him on Monday, but being with Maria had been just what the doctor ordered. What would it be like, he wondered, if they never had to say good-bye. What if he could spend every Sunday night in Trinity Springs, get up the next morning, and drive ten minutes to his office across the street from the courthouse.

It was an idea that a few weeks ago would have made no sense at all to him, but now…now it didn't seem so inconceivable.

Chapter Thirty-Two

Will noon ever get here? This is the longest morning I can remember since I had to endure boring contract law classes, Lucas thought as he struggled to find things to do to make the time pass faster. This was Monday—the day he would try to talk to his mother. He'd always wondered why she didn't just come home with him. Mama Rosa and Papa Joe would have taken her back in. He knew they would. But no. She'd chosen to leave and never talk to her parents or son again.

At least she had touched base with Isabel a few times. He could finally get some closure—not to mention the ability to probate Mama Rosa's will. That had been hanging over his head too long, and he wanted to get on with his life.

The phone in his pocket vibrated and startled him. "Hi, Maria."

"I didn't know if you'd be busy, but I thought I'd just leave a message if you didn't answer. Can you talk a minute, or do you want to call me back later?"

"I can talk. It's good to hear your voice. I'm a bundle of nerves."

"You're going to call your mother at noon, right?"

"It's hard to think of her as my mother, but yeah."

"I wanted to run something by you real quick. Mama called this morning to see if we would like to go to their house Saturday for a meal. Paul is taking a couple of the homeless vets to the lake for some fishing with Daddy, and Mama is looking forward to cooking for them and us. It'll be just two of them."

"Well, I…"

"Lucas, I'm sorry. This was a really bad time to call. Think about it when you don't have so much on your mind, and you can call me later. I'll be praying for you at noon."

"Thank you. And I'll probably be able to go to your parents' house Saturday, but we can talk later. I'll let you know how my phone call goes."

The rest of the morning plodded along tediously for Lucas, but when twelve o'clock arrived, he rushed out of the office and headed for his apartment fifteen minutes away. He could make the call, grab a quick sandwich, and be back in the office in an hour.

When he arrived at his apartment, he sat down at the table and took a deep breath. *It's now or never.* Ever so slowly, with a sweaty palm, he took Carmen's contact information out of his pocket and punched in the number.

"Bizzy Bee Cleaning Services. We clean while you rest. How may I direct your call?"

How may I direct your call? Lucas's first impression was that the company was bigger than he had imagined. "May I speak with Carmen Wilson, please?"

"Just a moment. I'll see if she's in her office."

After a wait that seemed to span several lifetimes, Lucas heard his mother's voice for the first time in almost twenty-five years.

"Carmen Wilson speaking."

Deep breath. "Ms. Wilson, this is Lucas Avila." Dead silence. Another long wait. "Ms. Wilson, are you there?"

"I'm here." He could hear her breathing on the other end. "I wondered when I would hear from you."

Lucas swallowed the lump in his throat before he was able to continue. Emotions were churning inside him that he hadn't expected. After some self-talk he regained control. "I'm calling to give you some news. Nothing more." Nothing more? That wasn't quite true, but he was trying desperately to keep this conversation businesslike.

"How *are* you?"

"How *am* I? I'm fine, thank you. Great, in fact." Hoping he'd made his point, he cleared his throat and continued. "I'm calling on behalf of both Isabel and myself to let you know that Papa Joe passed away three years ago, and Mama Rosa passed away six months ago. You're listed in her will to receive one-third of the estate. I'm executor of her will, and it can't be probated until you sign some papers. They also have to be notarized. May I have someone bring them to your office?"

"They're both gone…" Her voice, hesitant and barely audible, trailed off, almost as if she was letting the news sink in. Giving it time to register. And Lucas wondered if she had regrets.

"Yes, ma'am. They are."

"Well."

"Ms. Wilson, would it be all right if I send someone to your office with the papers you need to sign? I'll send a notary, but you will need to have two witnesses present also. You name the time. I know you have a busy schedule." A little dig, but he didn't really regret it.

"I'll sign them, of course, but you bring them. We need to talk."

"No, ma'am, we don't."

"Okay. We don't *need* to talk, but I'd like to. Would you at least think about it?"

Lucas tapped his fingers on the table as he considered how to answer. "I'll think about it and get back to you. I do actually have some questions."

"How did you locate me, Lucas?"

"I retained the services of a private detective because I needed these papers signed in order to probate."

"I see."

"I'll have my assistant draw them up, and then I'll be back in touch to arrange a time."

On Tuesday morning, Lucas and his notary entered the office of the owner and CEO of Bizzy Bee Cleaning Services. Despite his weak knees, he managed to maintain his composure at the first sight of his mother. "Ms. Wilson, I'm Lucas Avila with the law offices of Benson and Hughes, and this is Darla Green. She will notarize the papers you sign. You'll need a picture ID and two witnesses. Have you made arrangements for those?"

"I just need to call them in." Without taking her eyes off of Lucas, Carmen picked up the phone on her desk and punched a button. "Bev, send Ted and Grace to my office."

The signing went off without a hitch, Darla and the Bizzy Bee employees left, and Lucas was finally alone with the woman who had walked out of his life. This meeting scenario had played in his mind so many times, but he'd always imagined himself fully in control of his thoughts, his emotions. Now, he didn't even know where to begin. There were many questions he wanted answered, but which ones were the most important? Where should he even start?

For one thing, she didn't look like he had pictured her. She was older. Her chin-length black hair was showing signs of gray, there were a few wrinkles around her eyes, and her hands were the hands of a much older woman. A woman, he assumed, who had worked her way up to owning this company by cleaning houses. He'd always pictured her as looking a little like Isabel, but he realized now that he hadn't taken into consideration the seven years' difference in their ages.

She wore a rose-colored jacket over a white silk blouse and an impressive amount of jewelry. Large rings adorned two or three fingers on each of her hands. She had an intimidating look that Lucas suspected could control a subordinate with just a glance.

His mother spoke first, interrupting his thoughts. "So you're an attorney here in Dallas. That's wonderful."

"Thank you, Ms. Wilson, but…"

"Could you at least call me Carmen?"

"You said you wanted to talk. Do you have a question for me? Or should I start asking my questions?"

"Go ahead. Your questions will probably tell me everything I need to know. I'm sure you have a lot."

"First, I think I should tell you that I found my birth certificate a few weeks ago." His voice trembled slightly, and he found himself wishing he hadn't agreed to the meeting.

"Oh. That possibility never crossed my mind."

"Frankly, I'd never thought about it either. And if I had, I wouldn't have expected to see the name of my father there." He began to find his voice and continued.

"Why didn't you just put 'unknown'? Did you have a reason for identifying him after I was born?"

Carmen shifted in her seat and fidgeted with a couple of pens on her desk. Her obvious discomfort gave him no pleasure, but it didn't bother him, either. "That was so long ago," she said. "I wasn't thinking clearly. I don't remember now why I listed him. Is that significant to you?"

"What? Of course it's significant to me!" A frown appeared on Lucas's face.

"I suppose I can understand that. Have you done anything about it?" She stared across the desk at him, her eyes wide and questioning.

"I have actually."

"You've located him too?"

"Not exactly." He paused, partially to let her wonder for a few seconds and partially to think about how much information he wanted to give her. "But I've located my grandfather. Which leads me to my next question."

"Okay."

"My father. Did he know?"

"About you?" She shook her head. "No. I never told him."

"You mean you were carrying his child and you didn't think he deserved to know?" He took a deep breath, trying to control the anger that was building up inside him. "Help me understand that line of thinking."

"It was a complicated situation on many levels, Lucas." She hesitated, seeming to be deep in thought. "How much do you know about your father?"

"I know he's the son of one of the wealthiest families in Dallas. That, however, is not important to me."

"It was important to me, though." She held her hand up, palm facing him. "Not in the way you might think. I didn't want anything from them, but I knew that the woman who cleaned their house would never be accepted as the wife of their son or the mother of their grandchild.

Things might be different now, but when you were born, that's the way it was. I knew enough about that family to know they would have rejected me as the mother of their grandchild...and they probably would have rejected you too. And what about now? You said you've located your grandfather. Have you met him?"

"I have. He asked me to take a DNA test, and I did."

"But you haven't met Everett?"

"No."

"Why is that?"

"No one knows where he is. He apparently left home years ago and hasn't been heard from since." Lucas paused for effect again. "Kind of like you." He narrowed his eyes and stared straight into her dark brown ones.

"I understand your bitterness, Lucas. You might not think I do, but I do. All I can say is this. I thought I was doing what was best for you at the time. I had to work to support both of us, and it had gotten to the point where I couldn't take you with me to most of my jobs, and I couldn't afford to get a sitter. There was no other option. At least that was my thought, and I knew Mama and Papa would love you and give you a proper home. They did, didn't they?"

"I had a good life, but there were always unanswered questions. Sometimes I could push them to the back of my mind. Sometimes I couldn't."

"Of course."

"So you and Everett met when you were cleaning his parents' house? Was he living there at the time?"

"Yes and yes. He was just back from Kuwait. He was kind of a mess really. Such a tender soul to have had to witness the atrocities of war. Leaving him was not easy—just like leaving you was not easy—but I believed, at least at the time, that it was the only option."

"He fought in the Gulf War? That's the first I'm hearing about that." Lucas had always admired and respected military veterans, and knowing his father was one made him all the more determined to find him.

"Yes. He did. We met shortly after he came back."

"I didn't know. Do you have any idea where he might have gone when he left home?"

"None whatsoever. I didn't… I didn't know he'd disappeared. Never tried to find him again. I thought it best to leave it alone." She swallowed hard. "The truth is…I loved him deeply, but I had to make a clean break and build a life for myself without him."

Lucas rose. "I need to get back to the office, but for the record, I think you made a very selfish decision by not telling him he was going to have a child. It could have made a huge difference in his life. But we'll never know now, will we? Thank you for your time. I'll get back in touch when the probate is complete." And with that he exited the office.

Chapter Thirty-Three

Lucas punched in Maria's number as soon as he imagined she'd had time to get home and go for her run in the evening. "Hi. Sorry I didn't call last night. I worked late so I could take off a couple of hours this morning. How was your day?"

"Good. Nothing out of the ordinary happened. You?"

"I guess you would call it out of the ordinary when a guy is face-to-face with his biological mother for the first time in almost twenty-five years."

"I would say that isn't a commonplace occurrence. So? How did it go?"

"Not great. I asked her if Everett knew she was pregnant, and she said no. Can you imagine that? She was pregnant with his child, and she didn't even have the courtesy to tell him. She just vanished from his life. Like she did mine. It seems to be a thing with her. Get yourself in an uncomfortable situation and leave. Leave anyone who ever meant anything to you. Just go off and work your way up from a woman who cleans houses to owning a company, which, by all appearances, is doing quite well. It's all about her."

"Wow. I didn't expect it to be that bad. I'm so sorry, Lucas. Did she sign the papers you need to probate?"

"Yeah. She apparently didn't know Mama Rosa and Papa Joe had died. She seemed surprised, but other than that, I didn't see much emotion. She's very stoic."

"Are you planning to see her again?"

"I hope not. I think I'll have a courier take her the final papers."

"So you're cutting her off? Like she cut you off? As a way of getting back at her?"

"I don't know, Maria. I just have no desire to ever see her again. But enough about that. Let's change the subject. I wanted to tell you that I'll be happy to go to the lake with you Saturday, if the invitation still holds."

"Of course it does."

"And don't forget our date Friday night."

"I'm looking forward to it. Do you want me to meet you there?"

"Are you kidding? This is a proper date, ma'am. I'm coming to Trinity Springs to pick you up. Can you be ready by five? We have dinner reservations for six-thirty. I can't wait for you to meet Cooper. He and his date aren't joining us for dinner, but our seats are together at the theater."

"I'll be ready at five."

Clad in a brown sport coat and a light blue shirt, Lucas hopped out of his newly washed and waxed car and strode up the walkway to Maria's front door at exactly five o'clock on Friday afternoon. Before his hand touched the door to knock, Maria opened it with a flourish. "I saw you when you drove up. I mean I wasn't eagerly watching for you or anything," she said with an impish grin.

"Wow! You look... I mean... You look... Incredible. Stunning. Breathtaking. I can't seem to come up with the right word, but wow! That dress is beautiful, and so are you! Red is definitely your color. One of them anyway."

"Thank you, kind sir. You look pretty dashing yourself. I never thought I'd look this forward to going back to Dallas, but I'm really excited about the dinner and the musical."

"I hope it lives up to your expectations," Lucas said. "Otherwise, I'll really have to get my brain in gear to plan something for next time."

"You're assuming there will be a next time?" Maria winked and slipped her arm though his.

"Oops! Maybe I should have added 'I sure hope there will be a next time.'"

"Oliver's!" Maria exclaimed as Lucas pulled the car into the valet lane at the restaurant. "I've heard of it, but I've never been here. Nice touch. Based on this alone, there will be a next time." She smiled and added quickly, "But don't think I expect this again. I've been happy with our picnics."

"Me too. I think my favorite was the one in your closet." Lucas detached the key from his key fob and handed it to the valet.

"The closet picnic ranks right up there at the top for me too," Maria said. Lucas took her hand and squeezed it gently.

"Reservations for Avila," he said as they entered the restaurant and approached the hostess stand.

"This way, sir." She seated them at a table for two with a white tablecloth and a small arrangement of fresh flowers in a cut glass vase. Violin music played in the background. "Your server will be with you shortly."

Shortly was an understatement. A man in black slacks, a white shirt, and black vest was standing by the table as soon as they were both seated.

"Would you care for a cocktail or a glass of wine?"

"Just water for me, please," Maria said.

"I'd like a glass of iced tea. Are you sure you don't want something else, Maria?"

"No. Water's great. And maybe some lemon?"

"Sure. I'll give you a few minutes to look over the menu."

Maria had pondered whether to bring up Lucas's visit with his mother. On one hand, she didn't want to make him uncomfortable, but on the other hand, she didn't want him to think she wasn't interested. It was a huge event in his life, and if she had been in his shoes, she would want the chance to talk about it with someone who cared.

She decided to forge ahead—carefully. "We never really got a chance to talk about your visit with your mother. Do you want to talk about it?"

"I don't think of Carmen Wilson as my mother, but what do you want to know?"

"What you're thinking and feeling now that you've had time to process. You don't have to talk about her if you don't want to, but meeting Carmen was a huge event in your life. If it was me, I'd want a chance to hash through my emotions with someone who cares."

Lucas's features set like concrete. "I don't know that she's worth the effort of getting emotional over. Did you ever have a teacher in school who seemed unapproachable? You could tell she didn't want to be there? Didn't like kids at all? Thought only of herself and what she could get out of the job? Kept looking at the clock and hoping the bell would ring soon? That's the type of person she seems to me. I don't think she ever wanted to have a family. She was probably upset when she found out she was pregnant and happy when she dropped me off in Trinity Springs. She apparently came straight back to Dallas and started building her very profitable business. She probably never gave me a second thought."

"Are you sure about that? Didn't you say she got in touch with Isabel a few times to see how you were?"

"Out of curiosity, not love. If she had cared, she would have tried to see me. She would have helped Mama and Papa pay for college and law school. Goodness knows—from the looks of her business…and her—she could have afforded it better than they could. I'm sorry if I sound bitter…and I don't want to put a damper on our evening, but you asked."

"I asked because I wanted to know. And I wanted to know because I care. Thanks for telling me how you really feel. I didn't want you to sugarcoat it. I want us to be able to be honest and open with one another."

"And that's great. It is. I want that too," he said, "but let's talk about something else tonight."

They were about twenty minutes into their meal when two men approached their table. One appeared to be around their age, and the other one looked to be in his fifties or sixties. The younger of the two stopped beside them. "Maria… Hi. I certainly didn't expect to see you here."

"Peter. Um… Hi. I didn't expect to see you here either."

The older man had turned and taken a couple of steps back to the table. "You remember my dad, right?"

"Of course. Hello, Dr. Bernard. This is my friend, Lucas Avila."

"What are you doing back in Dallas?" Peter asked. "I thought you had left never to return. Never mind. I'm sorry to interrupt your dinner. We need to catch up, Maria. I'll give you a call. Pleased to meet you, Lucas."

"Who was that?" Lucas asked Maria when the two men were out of earshot.

"Just someone I knew when I lived here." She shrugged off the question with a light tone.

"Seemed like more than a casual friend. And you know his dad?"

"Long story," she answered, certain she didn't want to get into it tonight. "Not very interesting, though. And to borrow a phrase from you, let's talk about something else."

"And to borrow a phrase from you," he said, tossing her his signature crooked grin, "I want us to be able to be open and honest with one another."

"Touché," she said, but she wasn't smiling. In fact, the prime rib that had tasted so good a few minutes ago had lost its flavor.

Maria seemed to be in a daze for the rest of the evening. Lucas knew it must have something to do with the man in the restaurant, but that topic of conversation was apparently off the table. So he laid it aside and decided to try to enjoy the time he had with Maria.

Chapter Thirty-Four

Livvy Vargas had just taken the tamales out of the steamer on Saturday when the front door flew open and Lucas and Maria bounded into the kitchen.

"Whoa. Let me get those for you," Lucas offered, picking up the heavy bag of tamales. "They smell so good!"

"Sure smells better than that kale drink I had for breakfast," Maria said.

"What wouldn't?" Lucas shrugged and cut his eyes at Livvy after he'd set the tamales down on the granite countertop. "Kale's for rabbits. Right, Livvy?"

"It's certainly not for me. That I can tell you." She shook her head and grimaced. "Maria, why don't you call your dad and the other guys in? Tell them it's time to eat."

"What else can I do?" Lucas asked.

"You can get that big bowl of salad out of the refrigerator and put those wooden salad bowls on the table." She scooped up the tamales and put them on a platter. "And then put these on the table, along with the queso and red chili sauce." She laughed. "You might think twice about asking what you can do to help next time. You're probably getting more than you bargained for."

"Not at all. I like to work in the kitchen. I had a brief stint in a restaurant when I was in college."

"Well, when you finish all that, why don't you go out back and meet our guests. They should be off the lake by then."

Rob and the guys had been fishing for an hour, and Shane and Benny had each caught a medium-sized bass—just large enough to be called a keeper and fit for a fish fry. They began rowing the boat in when Maria called to her dad. "Hey, y'all! We're here, and Mama has lunch ready!"

Lucas and Maria were standing on the dock when Rob pulled up the boat, tied it, and helped Shane and Benny out. "These guys each caught a fish. I think they're naturals."

"Yep," Shane said. "I ain't been fishing since my grandpa took me when I was about twelve or thirteen. What about you, Benny?"

"First time."

"What? Oh, I remember. You told me that. You caught on quick. Fished as good as I did, didn't he, Mr. Vargas?"

"Y'all please call me Rob. Mr. Vargas makes me think my daddy must be standing behind me. But yes. You were both fast learners. I think you know my daughter Maria. And this young man with her is our friend, Lucas Avila."

Lucas extended his hand, not worried this time that they hadn't washed up after handling minnows and bass. Shane walked over and gave Lucas a hardy handshake. "Hi, there, Mr. Lucas. Hello, Miss Maria. Are you gonna sing for us again? You have a might pretty voice. I remember the time you sang for us in Dallas. Remember, Benny? She sang a special song for you."

Lucas looked at the other man who hadn't offered to shake his hand. It seemed as though the blood had completely drained from his face, and he put his hand on the wall to brace himself. Maria had apparently noticed too because she said, "When you guys get washed up, we'll eat. Daddy, why don't you show them where to go."

"What is wrong with you, Benny?" Shane asked as soon as they were out of earshot. "You look like you've seen a ghost."

Benny leaned against the closed bathroom door. "What did that young guy say his name was?"

"Wasn't it Lucas?"

"His last name."

"I don't know. Is it somebody you used to know? He seems too young. I ain't never seen him on the street. He don't look the type anyway."

"Was it Avila?"

"That sounds about right. Why?"

"I need to know." Benny's face filled with heat, and he tried to regain his composure. "Can you find out? You talk a lot. See if you can find out."

"All right. I'll try. But why?"

"Just find out if you can. I used to know a woman whose last name was Avila. And I just remembered she was from Trinity Springs." Benny stared into space. "But that was a lifetime ago." He managed to make it to the sink and let the water run over his hands for a long time. Then he splashed cold water on his face.

"Okay, buddy. I'll see what I can do," Shane offered, "but I don't want to be rude. These folks done took us fishing and they're gonna feed us a real meal. That don't happen too often, ya know."

As soon as they had washed up, Shane and Benny joined the others around the table. Shane sat down by Rob first, and the only seat left for Benny was by Lucas. He eased himself down on the chair slowly, trying not to make it obvious that he was unsettled.

"We say grace before we eat. I'll say it," Rob said as he held out his left hand to Shane. Benny looked around and saw that everyone was holding hands around the table. Glancing to his left, he noticed Lucas's hand ease over toward his. Not wanting to be the only one around the table not getting into the act, he anxiously moved his hand toward the young man's.

As their hands touched, electricity seemed to shoot through Benny's body, and he jerked slightly. *Compose yourself, Benny. It's a common name. Just a coincidence, that's all. They probably don't even know each other.*

Self-talk didn't do much to calm his nerves, and he wasn't able to fully enjoy the meal. The tamales tasted so good, though, and he wanted to box them up and take them to Dallas with him, to eat when he was back in familiar surroundings and not sitting next to someone whose last name was Avila. But he would never ask to do that.

The Vargases and Lucas were keeping the conversation lively, but Shane remembered what his friend had asked him to do and spoke up. "Did you say your name was Lucas?"

"That's right."

"And I don't think I caught your last name."

"Avila."

"Oh, that's right. I don't know what's wrong with me. I remember now. How do you know Maria?"

"We lived across the street until we were seven, but then the Vargases moved to Dallas. I grew up here in Trinity Springs. She moved back recently, and we got reacquainted. I work in Dallas now, but I come back here on weekends."

"Lucas is an attorney," Livvy added. "We're real proud of him. We were friends with his grandparents for many years."

Benny squirmed in his chair and continued to push the food around on his plate. He managed to take an occasional bite, but the queasy feeling lingered.

"That's cool," Shane replied. Then, probably to keep the focus on Lucas for Benny, he asked, "Are you two sweet on each other?"

Lucas and Maria looked at one another and grinned, and Rob laughed out loud.

"Shane!" Benny admonished.

"Oops. I didn't mean to overstep. I apologize. Sometimes I don't have much of a verbal filter. At least that's what Benny tells me, don't you, Benny?"

"Yes." He looked down and shook his head. Shane's comments were a constant source of surprise and amusement.

Shane continued. "Well, Lucas, since you live in Dallas, you should come visit us sometime. Our door is always open." He laughed. "Our door… Get it?"

To keep the joke from falling flat, the others around the table laughed too.

"Shane, I don't think this young man has time to come visit us," Benny inserted. "I'm sure he stays busy with his job."

"I do," Lucas replied, "but I just might take you up on that invitation. Maybe I'll come with Maria the next time she sings with her church group."

"Really?" Maria's face lit up and she smiled at Lucas. "I hope so!"

"Maybe we'll make it a family affair," Livvy added. "I'll bet I could talk my husband into taking his fiddle and singing a song or two with his daughter."

He wasn't sure what it was—maybe the easy way this family made conversation, so foreign to him…maybe the talk of music—but Benny found himself gradually relaxing and regaining his appetite. And the woman from so long ago retreated again to haunt the distant corners of his memory.

"Rob," Livvy said, noticing that Benny was finally eating, "pass the tamales around again. I think it's time for everyone to get a second helping. You guys will have to come back when Rob cooks those fish you caught today."

"Oh, yes, ma'am. We will, won't we, Benny?"

"We don't want to impose."

"It's not imposing," Rob said. "There's nothing like a good old fish fry out in the backyard. But it will have to be soon, or the temperature outside will be as hot as fish grease if we wait too much longer."

"Yes, sir," Shane piped up again. "We know how hot it gets, but we like summer better than winter."

"Oh, my! I was about to forget dessert." Livvy jumped up and headed for the kitchen. "Paul will be here soon to take you guys back to Dallas, but we can't let you leave yet."

As soon as Livvy had left the table, there was a knock on the door. "That's probably Paul," Rob said, as he got up to answer it. "I hope he'll stay and have pie with us."

Benny looked at Shane and squirmed in his chair, hopeful that his buddy would say something to make the moment less awkward.

Taking the cue, Shane spoke up. "We sure do hope you'll come to see us next time Maria comes down."

"I think I will," Lucas said. "And I've been meaning to thank you for your military service. I hear you're both veterans of the Gulf War. I have a keen interest in history. Of course, I don't know exactly what you went through over there, but I appreciate your volunteering to fight for our country."

Gulf War! Lucas tried to shake the thought from his head. Where had he heard that? Maria must have told him, but he was just now making the connection. Carmen had said Everett fought in the Gulf War. From his study of history, Lucas knew hundreds of thousands of troops were deployed in the early 1990s. It was too long a shot to think that the two guys he'd just met had even known an Everett Bennington, so he told himself to put that thought out of his mind.

"Hey, guys," Paul said as he entered the dining room. "I hear you both caught a fish."

"Paul," Livvy called from the kitchen, "you'll stay for pie, won't you? I'm sorry we're running a little bit late, but we've had a good time visiting around the table. And I think the guys enjoyed being on the lake."

"Sure. I wouldn't dream of leaving before pie. What kind did you make this time? Those apple pies you brought to Sherise's birthday party were delicious."

"I made buttermilk and pecan today." She set the tray containing the pies, dessert plates, and forks on the table. "Both fresh out of the oven."

"Count me in. No need to rush back, huh, guys?"

"Mrs. Vargas—" Shane started.

"Livvy, please, Shane."

"Well, you went to a lot of trouble, and we don't want to be rude. Ain't that right, Benny?"

"Of course. And we appreciate all of this. You didn't have to do it."

"Our pleasure. We love having guests. Coffee, anyone? I just made a fresh pot."

"Let me help you with the coffee, Mama," Maria said.

"That's okay. I can—"

"No, I'd like to."

"Okay..."

Maria followed her mother into the kitchen. "I need to tell you something, and there hasn't been a good time."

Livvy looked at her daughter and raised an eyebrow. "What's going on?"

"Lucas and I ran into Peter at Oliver's last night."

"Peter? Oh, my. Awkward?"

"It wouldn't have been if he'd just said hi and gone on, but he stopped at our table and said he'll call me so we can catch up. Like we need to catch up." Maria shrugged her shoulders and rolled her eyes. "Lucas was curious, of course."

"So I assume you haven't told Lucas you were engaged."

"I didn't see any reason to. That chapter of my life is closed."

"I know that and you know that, but Lucas doesn't know that. You'll have to tell him. Otherwise, he could think it's more than it is."

"As far as I'm concerned, he doesn't have to know about the engagement at all."

"I think you're playing with fire by not telling him everything, but it's your decision."

Chapter Thirty-Five

The call that changed everything for Lucas came midafternoon on Sunday. He'd touched base with Thomas Bennington Thursday to make him aware of his conversation with Carmen. They'd agreed to meet in a few days to debrief. Lucas heard his cell vibrate on top of the bureau in his bedroom on Bailey Street as he was going through his closet and trying to decide which of his old jeans were still in good enough condition to donate.

"Son," Thomas said as soon as he answered, "I want to hear about your meeting with your mother, but I've also been thinking about something that I'm sure will impact your life tremendously. I'd like to fill you in as soon as possible. Could we meet this evening?"

Lucas eased down into the closest chair and wiped his free hand across his forehead. His heart was racing and his mind replayed the words *will impact your life tremendously*. "I'm in Trinity Springs right now, but I planned to come back to Dallas this evening. I can leave now if it's important."

"It's important. Could we meet around five at Texas Prime on McKinney Avenue?"

"I can do that. You've piqued my curiosity, though. Can you tell me what this is about?"

"You father, Lucas. It's about your father. But I don't want to discuss it over the phone. I'll see you at five o'clock."

"Yes, sir. I'll be there." Lucas rose, dropped his phone into his pocket, and began to pace. *What could it be? Has Max found him too? He located Carmen pretty easily. That has to be it. Max has tracked down Everett Bennington, and Thomas decided to give me the information. Don't get your hopes up, Lucas. He might not live around here. He might be married and have a family somewhere. He might not even be alive.*

Lucas couldn't keep his mind from playing out endless scenarios. But there was one he wouldn't let himself entertain: His father lived close, didn't know he had a son, and would be eternally grateful to meet and get to know him. That was too much to hope for. When that one popped up, he managed to shove it to the back of his mind.

He had driven a little too fast to get to Trinity Springs a few times, but never to get back to the city. There was a lot riding on this meeting, though. Thomas wouldn't have called him back on Sunday evening and asked to meet him somewhere besides his office if it wasn't something of great significance. The essential question that loomed large in Lucas's mind was *Has my father been located?* And the only answer he could come up with was *Yes*. What other development could have caused his grandfather to summon him back to Dallas immediately?

Pulling into the Texas Prime parking lot at 4:55, Lucas promptly recognized Max's BMW. He wasn't surprised. Max had played an important role in the search for both Carmen and Everett. Why shouldn't he be here?

The detective was waiting for him by the hostess stand and led him to a private U-shaped booth in the back of the restaurant where Thomas was working on what appeared—from the looks of the empty glass in front of him—to be his second martini.

"Sit down, son. Thanks for meeting at the last minute. We'll order dinner shortly, but Max will get you a drink at the bar. What'll it be?"

"Just iced tea for me. Thanks."

"Not a drinker, huh?"

"Not usually. I like to keep my head clear. Especially when it seems we're going to discuss an important topic."

"That we are, my boy. That we are. Did you have much traffic on the way down?"

Max sat the iced tea down in front of Lucas and he took a long swig. "Not too bad today."

"Let's get right to it then. Shall we? Why don't you start by telling us how your visit with your mother went."

Lucas was antsy to get information concerning Everett, but he'd told Thomas he'd let him know how the meeting with Carmen had gone, so apparently the main reason for this discussion would have to wait.

"I have a hard time referring to her as my mother, so I'm going to call her Carmen."

Thomas nodded, sipped his drink, and ate the olive off the end of the toothpick. "Whatever works for you."

"I called her on Monday, told her I needed her signature on some papers in order to probate the will, and went to her office on Tuesday. She didn't know about the passing of my grandparents."

"And she hadn't seen you since you were three years old?"

"No, sir. Not that I know of."

"Go on."

A server appeared at the table, and Thomas ordered for all three of them. "I hope you don't mind, but I never met a man who didn't like a thick rib eye steak and baked potato."

"No. That sounds great."

"Continue with your visit with your…with Carmen."

"She and Everett met right after he had come back from Kuwait and she was cleaning your house. When she found out she was pregnant, she left and went back to Trinity Springs. She never told him. He doesn't know about me. That's why I'm more determined than ever to locate him. I think she made a huge mistake by keeping her pregnancy a secret, and I told her as much."

"Do you plan to see her again?" Thomas asked.

"I have no desire to. I can get a courier to take the papers to her office when the probate is complete. By the way, she's not cleaning houses anymore. She owns the company. And it seems to be quite a booming business."

"It is. It's worth a lot of money. I had Max look into it."

Max, sitting directly across from Lucas, just grinned and nodded his head.

Thomas continued. "As you know, Max is very good—I'd venture to say the best in Dallas—at obtaining information. Sometimes it takes him a while, but he always comes through. He's been working for me for many years and has proven to be my most valuable asset and completely trustworthy."

"It's amazing that he got that information out of my aunt. She would never have given it to me, so I'm grateful."

Thomas put a hand on Lucas's shoulder. "Prepare to be even more grateful."

Max hadn't said a word but continued to stare at Lucas and display that mischievous grin.

"What do you mean, sir? You said this meeting was about my father. What do you know?"

"Max, why don't you take over," Thomas said. "This is your baby now. You've earned it."

"Thanks, Mr. B. Lucas, when you first made your presence known to your grandfather, he asked me to look into you. To see if maybe you were trying to scam him.

With people of his, shall we say, social standing, it's not entirely unheard of to run into people who would want to take advantage. Instead, I found you to be—what were the words I used, Mr. B?—squeaky clean, I think. We both felt you were the real deal. And I might add that he was quite impressed that you couldn't be bought with a promise of $50,000 a year."

"Max, I'm going to cut in here for just a minute. Lucas, before he tells you any more, I want to sincerely apologize to you. First for trying to buy you off. And second for telling you a lie."

"A lie?" Lucas leaned back in the booth, his eyes searching Thomas's face for answers.

"Continue, Max."

"Mr. B was trying to protect his son—along with his wife and his other son—so he told you he didn't know where Everett was."

"But you *do*?" Anger rose inside of Lucas. "You let me go this whole time thinking you didn't know where he is?" His voice was noticeably louder, and he glared at his grandfather incredulously. "Why would you do that when you knew how much it meant to me to locate him?"

"It wasn't right." Thomas said. "I know that now, but when you learn the circumstances, you might begin to understand. I hope so anyway."

Lucas tried to control his breathing as Max continued. "Lucas, Everett left the family a few years after returning from Kuwait. He left them only this note." Max handed him a folded, dog-eared piece of paper, and gave Lucas a minute to read it.

When Lucas finally looked up, Max continued. "The family assumed it was because of the PTSD he had suffered, as had so many other men and women who return from war, but we suspect now that was only part of the reason. You've just confirmed that Carmen's leaving abruptly might have contributed to his confused state of mind."

"So cut to the chase, Max," Lucas pleaded. "Where is my father? When can I see him?"

"I've instructed Max to take you to him," Thomas cut in. "You deserve to know who your father is, and he deserves to know he has a son. There's something you need to understand, though, and there's no easy way to tell you this. Just as there was no easy way for Max to tell me when he finally found Everett fifteen years ago."

"What is it? Just spit it out, for goodness' sake!" Lucas was growing increasingly impatient with the whole situation.

Max straightened his shoulders and leaned in toward Lucas. "There's no way to sugarcoat it. Everett Bennington is homeless. You father left a comfortable home and family to live on the street for all these years. I have a photo of him that was taken right before he left home...apparently around the time he was secretly seeing your...seeing Carmen." He handed the photo to Lucas.

"*What? This is my father?*" No. It couldn't be. But the light blue eyes. That was one of the first things Lucas had noticed about Thomas when he sat across the desk from him the day he confronted him in his office. Lucas peered at his grandfather again. Benny had those same eyes. The young man in the photograph was wearing a military uniform. Benny and Shane both served in the army during Desert Storm. Hadn't Carmen mentioned Kuwait when she was talking about Everett? Everett Bennington. Benny. Lucas couldn't believe he'd been in the presence of his father and hadn't put all those pieces together. He was overwhelmed with the realization. Feeling lightheaded, he absentmindedly pushed his plate away.

"We knew it would come as a surprise to you," Thomas said. "I've had many years to get used to the idea that one of my sons, who could have had a huge stake in a very profitable company, chose—*chose*, Lucas—to live on the street. All these years I thought the terrors of war had changed him…had driven him away. Now I'm not so sure."

Lucas's brain was still reeling from trying to process the situation. Not the fact that he now knew where his father was. But that he might have…probably had…already met him. If ever there was an example of irony, he thought, this was it.

Chapter Thirty-Six

The way Benny had reacted when he heard Lucas's last name. At first Lucas thought he'd imagined it. That the man was just uncomfortable and felt out of place in a home...away from everything familiar. But now. With this new information, with the photo...

"You won't believe this," Lucas said when he could find his voice again, "but yesterday I was with two homeless veterans. A pastor from Trinity Springs brought them to my friends' house on Cypress Grove Lake to go fishing. Their names were Shane"—Lucas paused—"and Benny." He scanned the faces of the two men sitting in the booth with him for some confirmation of his suspicion.

This time it was Thomas and Max's turn to be shaken. Max recovered first and spoke. "Lucas, you've apparently met your father already. He goes by 'Benny' on the street. This is spectacular. Who would've thought..."

Lucas began to tremble slightly and tried to swallow the lump in his throat. He didn't cry easily, but he couldn't keep tears from welling up in his eyes. Thomas's expression softened. He handed Lucas a handkerchief and reached over and put his hand on his grandson's shoulder.

"Son, when I called you here today, I never expected a coincidence like this. It's the last thing I would have imagined."

Lucas still was not able to speak. He kept shaking his head in disbelief.

Max leaned in and spoke softly. "Everett doesn't know we've located him, but I've been keeping an eye on him for about fifteen years. I report back to your grandfather periodically about his wellbeing. If we ever suspected he was in danger or needed anything or was discontent with being on the street, we would have swooped in. However, he never appeared to be in distress at all. Of course, we always hoped he would rejoin society, but he never gave any indication that was the case."

"But now? What do you think *now*?" Lucas asked with a shaky voice. "You said earlier he deserves a chance to know he has a son. That could make a big difference, right?"

"We've come to that conclusion," Max continued. "Learning about you might be just the impetus needed to turn his life around."

"It won't be easy, though." Thomas sighed. "He's been on the street almost as long as he wasn't. It seems to be where he's comfortable. Remember, it was his choice."

"That's what I don't understand." Lucas's brows drew closer together. "Why would he leave a…well, a comfortable home and everything he knew to have such a vastly different life?"

"Why would he leave?" Max shrugged. "We've asked that question hundreds of times. But now I think we have a better idea of a possible reason. Rejection? A lost love? Some things can have more devastating effects on people than we are able to conceive."

"Does…Does anyone else in the family know you located him?"

"No one else knows but Max and me," Thomas said. "I don't think Sally and Thomas Jr. would be able to live with knowing this and not being able to approach him with questions. He didn't want that. Well, you read the note. It was obvious to me he wanted to be left alone."

"But then I appear out of the blue," Lucas said, "and things are different."

"Definitely different." Max nodded and smiled.

"I'm probably going to surprise you both with my next statement," Lucas said, "but I really believe this is the best way to proceed."

"Of course, we want your opinion. You might have the biggest stake in this. Sally and I have grieved our loss for years, but you have a chance at a new beginning. The last thing you want to do is mess it up. What's your thought?" Thomas asked.

"Max should approach him, tell him about me, gauge whether he wants to see me. I won't force myself on him. It might help if he knows we've already met, though."

"That's not a bad idea. No matter how it happens, it will be a shock, I'm sure. He might need time to consider his options. Max," Thomas said, turning to his trusted detective, "are you up for this? I agree with Lucas. It might be better not coming from a family member."

"Sure, boss. It would be my pleasure. As you know, I've grown rather fond of Benny in the fifteen plus years I've been keeping an eye on him."

"Then Max will keep you posted, Lucas. I know we would all like to see something good come from this. I hope you can forgive me for withholding this information for so long."

"I know it's a complicated and heartbreaking situation for your family—and my showing up has added to the complexity—but I wish I'd known sooner."

"When you get to be my age, son, you can look back and see many times when you'd give anything if you had reacted differently to a situation. This is definitely one of those for me."

Lucas saw despair written all over Thomas's face and almost felt sorry for him. "Don't beat yourself up. You did what you thought was best for your family at the time. You didn't know me. And we can't forget about Carmen's contribution to this whole situation. It was wrong of her not to tell him she was pregnant. To just leave without telling him why." Lucas stared into space and shook his head. "I still can't believe I've already met him and didn't even know it."

"Sometimes the universe plays tricks on us like that," Max said. "I'll let you know as soon as I talk with him."

Lucas extended his hand across the table to both of the men. "Call me any time of the day or night. I'm going to head out. There's someone in Trinity Springs I need to talk to before tomorrow."

Once again there was little to no traffic on the highway from Dallas to Trinity Springs, and Lucas pressed down hard on the gas pedal. He needed to see Maria. To tell her that the homeless veteran she'd grown fond of was his father. The father he'd been searching for since he'd discovered the name on his birth certificate. What a turn of events this was! He still couldn't believe it himself, but it might make it seem more real if he shared it with someone. And of course that someone would have to be Maria. Their relationship had progressed to the point of his wanting to share everything with her.

He wheeled his Toyota into the gravel driveway at his house, jumped out of the car, and went inside for a minute to check himself in a mirror. Sometimes his hair needed a little attention, and he wanted to look his best when he saw her.

As he opened the door to dash across the street, a white Mercedes pulled up in front of Maria's house. The driver's side was facing Lucas, and he recognized the man getting out of the car as the guy they'd run into at Oliver's Friday night. Peter. The guy she'd tried to downplay.

"Just a friend," she'd said. But Lucas also remembered Peter had said, "We need to catch up." *So the guy lives in Dallas and drives all the way to Trinity Springs on Sunday evening to catch up?* Lucas didn't like the looks of it, but as badly as he wanted to talk to Maria, this didn't seem like the time to march across the street and confront her, so he closed his door, sidled over to the living room window, and pulled the curtain back a tiny bit.

Maria flung the door open at the knock, hoping it was Lucas. She'd been counting on seeing him before he went back to Dallas for the week. Weekends only didn't seem like enough anymore. The more she was with him, the more she wanted to be with him.

"Peter!" she gasped. "What… What are you doing here?"

"I told you I'd be in touch. So here I am. This is me being in touch."

"I assumed you meant you'd call. And when you called, I was going to tell you there's nothing more to say. We said it all over a year ago."

"Maybe we didn't say it all. Can I come in?"

"I don't know what you think you'll gain by—"

"Please. I won't stay long. After seeing you in Dallas Friday night, I felt like we needed to talk face to face."

"Okay, but don't expect anything to come from this. I've moved on with my life."

Peter stepped across the threshold, and Maria closed the door.

Chapter Thirty-Seven

Lucas had never felt so alone in his life. He'd just found out his father was one of the homeless guys he'd met at Cypress Grove, and the first person he wanted to confide in had a visitor. But not just any visitor. One whose unexpected appearance Friday night had made her noticeably uncomfortable. That wouldn't have happened if the guy were just a friend as she claimed. And that thought made *Lucas* uncomfortable.

So he picked up his phone, punched in the number of the woman who had always been a constant in his life, and slumped down into the nearest chair. "Hey, Sherise. You busy?"

"Just sitting down to watch a movie, but I'd rather talk to you."

Reassured at the sound of her cheerful voice, Lucas asked, "Do you mind if I come over?"

"I would love that. Are you okay?"

"It's been a day of highs, lows, and everything in between." He rubbed his temple with his free hand. "I guess I just need someone to talk to. And tag—you're it."

The Mercedes was still parked on the street in front of Maria's house when Lucas backed out of his driveway. In less than ten minutes he pulled up in front of Sherise's. When her husband died, she'd moved into her family home. By that time, her brother and sisters had moved out, and since her father needed fulltime skilled nursing care, he was moved to a facility in town where she made sure he was safe and comfortable until he passed away.

Lucas had always liked the house. Sherise had given it an updated look with new floors and fresh paint. It had Sherise written all over it and had always been a soft place for Lucas to land.

"Get in here and get a hug. Sounded like you need one." Sherise enveloped Lucas in the kind of healing embrace that had always managed to fill his emotional tank.

"A hug, an ear, a shoulder. All of the above."

"I believe your words were 'highs, lows, and everything in between,' so of course I'm curious. What gives?" she asked.

"You'd better sit down for this."

She lowered herself onto the nearest chair, and Lucas plopped down on the couch across from her.

"Would you believe I met my father yesterday?" he blurted. "And didn't know it until about an hour and a half ago."

"No way," she said, eyebrows raised. "Who? Where? How?"

Lucas filled her in on the lunch at Maria's parents' house and meeting Shane and Benny. About the phone call from Thomas and the meeting at Texas Prime.

Sherise took a moment to process what she'd just heard. "I don't know if that's the high or the low or the in between, but that's an almost unbelievable story. One for the books. Who would've thought?"

"Yeah. Novels have been written with less of a plot than this. It's hard to figure out why someone—even a war veteran who's been rejected by someone he apparently loved—would choose to leave all his worldly goods behind and live on the street. I don't get it."

"We have no way of knowing what goes on inside of people—what inner demons torment them. So he has no idea you're his son?"

"He doesn't even know he has a son. Carmen left without telling him she was pregnant."

Sherise shook her head in disbelief. "This is incredible, Lucas. I can't imagine what you must be feeling."

"That's not all."

"You have something that can top that?"

"I don't know if 'top' would be a word I'd use, but yeah. I've been on an emotional roller coaster for a few hours."

"You saw him again?"

"No. I hope to soon, but this is about Maria."

"Oh, thank goodness. I'm ready for some good news about you two."

"I wish I had some to give you. What do you know about Maria and a guy named Peter?"

Sherise slapped her hand to her forehead. "Oh, mercy! How do you know about *him*?"

"Well, you've just confirmed my worst suspicions. You know about him and I don't. Not a good sign. Who is he and what's he to Maria?" Lucas leaned in and focused fully on Sherise, awaiting her reply.

Sherise lifted her eyes and met Lucas's stare. "I wish I could set your mind at ease, Lucas, but it's not my story to tell. Have you asked Maria?"

"She said he's just someone she knew when she lived in Dallas, but if you know about him, it's obviously more than that." Lucas told Sherise about running into him and his father at Oliver's. "He's at her house as we speak."

"*Really?* I can't imagine she would have invited him. Did she know you were coming back and wanted to talk to her?"

"No. We've always just popped over."

"Lucas, Lucas, Lucas," she said shaking her head. "Have I taught you *nothing*? If you really care for Maria, you're going to have to pursue her a little more—how shall I put this?—respectfully. Show her some consideration. Give her a call first. Ask if it's a convenient time. What if you just popped over sometime and she had her hair up in curlers? That's an exaggeration—I don't imagine the younger generation uses curlers—but ladies want to look their best when they see someone they like. And sometimes that takes us a little longer than it takes you guys."

"I get it. I guess I've been taking her for granted."

"You're going to have to make that right, you know. And *soon*!"

"I know. I will. The funny thing is—don't you tell a soul about this, Sherise—but I was actually thinking about moving back to Trinity Springs and opening a practice here. You know that empty space on the square around the corner from the café?"

"Really? That's great news! You're as out of place in the city as an earthworm on a Texas sidewalk in August. I guess you finally figured that out."

"I thought I had a lot figured out, but it's been quite a day, and I'm not so sure now. Apparently the possibility of moving back had a great deal to do with Maria, so maybe it doesn't matter now."

"It matters. Yes, it does. More than you can imagine."

There were a million questions Lucas wanted to ask, but he knew Sherise would never betray a confidence—

even to him. Plus, he was beginning to fade and needed to drive back to the city while he was still capable of staying awake for another hour. "I'm gonna run, but thanks for letting me interrupt your movie."

"Don't think I won't follow up on this. You have to talk to her. Tell her you're planning to move back. I can't overstate the importance of that decision, Lucas. You've made an old woman very happy…and you'll make a young woman even happier. I know what I know," she said, a sly smile playing across her face.

Lucas was back in his Dallas apartment late Sunday night, thinking about what he had told Sherise about moving to Trinity Springs, and for the life of him, he couldn't imagine where that had come from. He *had* entertained the thought a few times, and he *had* noticed a For Lease sign in an empty office space on the square, but he hadn't given a move *serious* consideration. Hadn't thought about quitting Benson and Hughes and giving up a steady salary. Hadn't contemplated leaving his apartment and moving back into his childhood home.

But now that he'd voiced the idea to Sherise…well, it didn't sound so bad. He'd enjoyed weekends away from the city more than he could have imagined a few months ago. When he was in high school, his thoughts had centered on getting a law degree and leaving Trinity Springs as quickly as possible. Striking out on his own in Dallas…or maybe another large city. He'd considered Austin, Houston, and even Oklahoma City or Tulsa.

If he were being honest, though, he'd have to admit that big-city life wasn't all it was cracked up to be. There were plusses, sure. Restaurants and entertainment. New people to meet. A good job with benefits. But did those things outweigh the familiarity of his hometown? People he'd known all his life? Fresh country air? A drop-dead-gorgeous across-the-street neighbor?

According to Sherise, there was still hope for a relationship with Maria. She'd been genuinely reassuring. But when he thought about Peter, he wasn't so optimistic. It hadn't looked promising when he'd gone back home before leaving for Dallas and the Mercedes was still parked in front of Maria's house.

Chapter Thirty-Eight

During winter, when Benny was camped out under the bridge and not within walking distance of the Dallas Public Library, he missed the leisurely stroll to his favorite hangout. But today was as fine a Monday morning as he could hope for, and his walk was particularly pleasant. Flowers grew in profusion in squares of dirt around trees planted in the middle of the sidewalk, and he prided himself on being able to name each species he saw. In years past, if he happened to spot a flower he didn't know, he'd take a plant book off the shelf and peruse each page until he found a picture of it and add it to his repertoire.

When Benny stepped off the elevator on the eighth floor, his favorite librarian waved, reached under her desk, and pulled out a biography he'd been reading for a few days. Although Hannah had allowed Benny and Shane to take out books on her library card, they'd decided not to do it again, afraid the books would get lost, stolen, or ruined by the weather. So he was back to reading in the library…and he didn't mind at all. This way he got to spend more time with someone who had come to mean a great deal to him. When she was sure her supervisor wasn't looking, she always managed to bring him a cup of coffee or a bottle of water.

On this particular morning, Benny had been reading for about thirty minutes when a man he didn't know approached his table and plopped down in a chair across from him. He glanced at the stranger briefly and then started reading again.

"Benny?" the man said softly.

Benny looked up. This guy was no one he recognized from the homeless community. No one from Paul's church. And as far as he could tell, he'd never seen the man before. He wore jeans and a plain navy T-shirt. A red Texas Rangers cap adorned his head. His clothes appeared to have been ironed or professionally laundered. This was no homeless guy.

Benny was leery but whispered, "Do you... Do you know me?"

"My name is Max McBride. I work for your father."

Benny tensed, closed his book, pushed his chair back, and started to stand.

"Please stay. I have some important news for you. I'll explain everything. There's nothing to fear. I'm not here to try to get you to come back. I just have information your father and I think you would want to know."

Slowly and haltingly, Benny eased back down in his chair. He glanced over toward Hannah's desk. She was looking his way. When their eyes met, she nodded and headed to his table.

"Sir," she said to Max, "is there something I can help you with? This gentleman doesn't seem to know you."

Max stood and tipped his cap to her. "Miss Hannah, I'm not here to harm anyone. I just need to talk to Benny. I know you care a lot about him and are trying to protect him, but I can assure you that I'm only trying to give him some information he will want to know."

Hannah stood ramrod straight and took a step back. "How do you know my name?"

Max handed her a business card. "I'm a private detective. I'm afraid that's all I can tell you, but Benny is free to tell you more if he chooses to later. As I said, I know—"

"It's okay, Hannah," Benny broke in.

"All right, but if you need anything…" She made eye contact with Max one more time before she headed back to her desk.

"She's pretty special to you, isn't she?" Max asked when she was out of earshot.

"Yes."

"Apparently the feeling's mutual."

"What information did you want to give me?" Benny asked. "And how did you find me?"

"I could tell you here, but it's a long story, and I'm kind of hungry. Would you mind if we go somewhere else? Have you had breakfast? I have an expense account I'm trying to use up for this month."

"Okay."

On his way out, Benny handed Hannah the book he'd been reading. "I'll see you again tomorrow. It's okay. We're going to get breakfast."

As Hannah reached out her hand for the book, she put her other hand around his wrist. "If I don't see you tomorrow morning—"

He gave her his signature crooked grin. "I'll be here."

Max and Benny found a café a block from the library. "Sit anywhere," the guy behind the counter called out. "Someone will take your order shortly."

"I'm going to have some pancakes and bacon. How about you?" Max asked Benny. "Or would you rather have eggs?"

"Pancakes."

When the server came to take their order, Max said, "Two large stacks of pancakes with lots of bacon and lots of syrup. Also, two coffees, cream and sugar on the side." Max looked at Benny with raised eyebrows. Benny nodded. "That'll be all," Max told the server.

As soon as they were alone again, Benny spoke up. "Why are you here? Why did my father send you after all these years? How did you find me?"

"As I told Hannah," Max began, "I'm a private detective, and I've been on retainer for your father for about twenty years…almost as long as you've been gone. I've done a lot of work for him—mostly vetting people he considered doing business with—but my most important task, by far, has been to locate you and make sure you were okay. Mr. B wanted to know you were safe. When I found you and reported that you seemed to be at peace here, that put his mind at rest. He told me to honor your request to leave you alone, but I've been checking on you for fifteen years. I report back to him every few months. He always wants to know if you seem to be happy and in good health. So far I've been able to give him positive reports, and he's been satisfied to not rock the boat."

"But you're rocking the boat now. Why?"

"There's been a new development that we both think you have a right to know."

"My mother and brother? Are they okay? I read the paper every day, and I haven't seen anything about anyone in the family being sick or in an accident."

"They're fine. Your mother and Thomas, Jr. don't know we've located you. Your father thought it best that way."

The server set steaming cups of coffee down in front of the men, and Max doctored his with both cream and sugar. Benny wrapped strong hands around his mug and took a sip. "Thank you for this."

"You can thank your father. He'll be glad I'm putting my generous expense account to good use."

"So, why—"

"Right. I'll get to the point. A few weeks ago, a young man went to see your father and presented him with a newly discovered birth certificate. It had your name on it as his father, and he wanted to know who you were and where you were."

Benny set his coffee down and leaned back in his chair. "No. That's impossible." He'd been with only one woman, the one he'd never been able to get out of his heart or his mind.

"That's what your father thought, so he asked him to take a DNA test."

"And?" She never told him she was pregnant. Surely she wasn't pregnant when she disappeared so unexpectedly.

"It came back with 99.9% accuracy." Max plucked the test results from his pocket and slid the paper across the table. "I know this is a shock, and I'm sorry to have to break it to you like this, but we couldn't think of any other way to give you the news."

Benny studied the paper and swallowed hard. "So you're telling me that I have a son I knew nothing about all this time?"

"Yes. And he knew nothing about you. Didn't know your name until he came across his birth certificate a couple of months ago."

"I don't believe it," Benny said, shaking his head. A baby? The idea was ludicrous. "She wouldn't have… Is that why she…?" Even as he denied it, memories of Carmen came unbidden to his mind. Bittersweet moments he'd long since set aside because dwelling on them hurt too much. She'd been so beautiful. So vivacious. So full of life. He'd never loved a woman as he'd loved her. He'd nearly worked up the courage to propose. Then she'd vanished from his life. No explanation. No forwarding address. She simply disappeared.

"That's why she left without telling you. The difference in social status of the two families. She felt she wouldn't be accepted by your parents. The baby wouldn't be accepted…"

"Do you know her?" Benny looked at Max, almost pleading with him for answers. Wanting him to erase the last thirty years and make everything make sense. Make it different.

"I haven't met her. She didn't raise your son, but he's located her and talked with her recently."

"Does she live here? In Dallas?" Had she been this close? All this time? Hope nudged him, despite his efforts to tamp it down. Possibilities he couldn't allow himself to articulate.

"That's a matter for you and your son to discuss. Assuming you want to meet him…"

Benny stared out the window for a long time, his eyes focused on images of long ago. He and Carmen had met right after he'd returned from Kuwait. He was vulnerable, and she'd filled a vacuum in his life at the time. He was living with his parents, trying to figure out what he wanted to do with the rest of his life, and he fell in love with the brown-eyed beauty. They managed to keep their relationship a secret, but Benny was thinking about asking her to marry him. He didn't care what his high-society parents thought about their son loving and starting a family with the woman who cleaned their house once a week. He was head over heels.

Benny wondered what she was like now. Was she still beautiful? Still sweet? Still soft and warm as she'd been in his arms?

So much time had passed, though. So many dreams had died. And he couldn't change any of it. Even if Carmen had been found. Better to leave the past to the past.

But he had a son. A son who'd come searching for him.

Max stayed silent and let him process. The server brought their food to the table.

Benny's eyes finally met Max's. "I want to meet him."

"We were hoping you would. He's a fine young man. Let's eat before our food gets cold." Max poured half a bottle of syrup on his pancakes and handed it to Benny.

"I can't believe it. How long have you and my father known about this?"

"For a few weeks, but we just located his mother recently."

"Carmen…Avila."

"Yes."

"Why didn't she raise him? Who did?"

"Her parents."

"Wait." Benny's heart started racing, and his voice cracked with emotion. "He has her last name and was raised by his grandparents?" It couldn't be. It couldn't! He stared at Max wide-eyed. "Is my son…"

"That's right. You've met him." Max put a photo of Lucas in front of him. "He didn't know you were his father on Saturday either, but he does now…and he wants to talk with you again soon."

Benny laid down his fork and put his hand over his mouth. His eyes grew red and moist. "I have a son. And he's a lawyer?" He brushed away a couple of tears that had escaped his eyes and run down his cheeks.

"Yes, and he's a fine young man."

"He knows I live on the street." A feeling of shame and regret washed over Benny.

"He does."

"I want to see Carmen. I have a lot of questions."

"I'm sure you do," Max said. "That's something you and Lucas can discuss."

"Lucas." It was the first time he'd spoken the name of his son, and the tears flowed freely.

Chapter Thirty-Nine

Lucas was in court Monday afternoon assisting Cooper with a case they'd been working on for weeks when his phone vibrated and a text message from Max popped up.

> Call me when you get a chance.

After thirty long minutes the judge finally recessed, and Lucas rushed out of the courtroom and into the hallway. "Hey, Max. What is it?"

"Can you get away early this afternoon?"

"Possibly. To do what?"

"Your father wants to meet you. Again."

"You've told him already? I didn't expect it so soon. Is he… How did he take the news?"

"Let me put it this way: He's already told about three-fourths of the people who camp out around him, and he's on his way to the library to tell his favorite librarian. By the way, Lucas, she's a real cutie. You might want to meet her."

"He believed you right away? Was he surprised you knew where he was?"

"He was leery at first. Took me a while to win him over, but I showed him the DNA test. I took him to a café for breakfast. We were there an hour. And Lucas, he wants to see Carmen."

"I figured he would. Let me call you when I get back to the office. My ride's waiting for me, so I need to run. I'll be in touch when I find out what time I can get away. Thanks for everything you've done, Max."

It was nearly four-thirty before Lucas was able to leave the office and go to his apartment to change from his suit into jeans and a short-sleeve shirt. Meeting his father for the first time since they both knew about the relationship was causing his stomach to churn and his head to reel with *what-ifs*. What if Benny expected more from Lucas than he was prepared to give? What if he didn't want or wasn't able emotionally to have an ongoing relationship with his newly acquired son? What if he thought his and Carmen's love affair could pick up where it left off?

That was the one that worried Lucas most of all. Max had said Benny wanted to see her. Lucas thought it would be his undoing. He feared she wasn't at all the way Benny remembered her when he was Everett Bennington of Bennington and Bennington Enterprises and she was the young woman who cleaned his parents' house.

He couldn't put it off any longer, though, so he headed downtown after punching the address Max had given him into his car's GPS. He recognized the street name as the part of town he usually avoided, but now it was his destination. How had it come to this? How had he gone in two short months from having a satisfying existence as a Dallas attorney to a man who no longer knew where he wanted to live and who was about to have his first one-on-one conversation with the father he never knew he had?

The more he thought about it, the more he suspected Mama Rosa had known all along he'd find his birth certificate and be curious enough to search until he found Everett Bennington. The same way she'd put Carmen in the will. She knew he'd have to locate her to probate. Yes, the fact that his grandmother had given him reasons and clues to come face-to-face with his roots was becoming a certainty in his mind.

Twenty minutes after leaving his apartment, Lucas was parking his car in front of a rundown auto-body shop and saying a silent prayer that it would still be there when he returned. He hadn't walked three feet when he spotted Shane and Benny sitting on the sidewalk and leaning against a graffiti-adorned wall.

Shane spotted Lucas first. "There he is, Benny!"

Benny shot to his feet and stuck out his hand. Lucas took it and said, "When we met on Saturday, I had no idea."

"I never knew about you. She didn't…"

"I know." Lucas waved to Shane, who was also standing but had stayed back, apparently to give them some space. "Hi, Shane. Good to see you again."

"You said you might come see us. Remember when I said our door is always open? Well, it is, isn't it?" Shane turned his hand up and moved it from his left to his right in a gesture that said to Lucas, *This is all ours. This is our open door and you are welcome.*

Lucas nodded and laughed. "Yes, and I appreciate the hospitality." He turned to Benny. "Is there somewhere we can talk in private?"

"We could go to the library," Benny said. "It's a fifteen-minute walk. Or there's a coffee shop around the corner. But you have to buy something if you go there. They don't let you just come in and sit."

"I could use a cup of coffee. Let's go there."

A crowd had begun to gather around them, and Shane was trying to shoo them away without much luck.

"This your boy, Benny?" a man called out. Benny nodded.

"That's Benny's son," another whispered to the woman standing beside him. "He didn't know he had a son until today."

"Is that right? Well, do tell."

"Let's go," Benny said to Lucas, and they rounded the corner.

Cup o' Joe was empty when they entered, and Lucas glanced at his watch. It was after five, and his stomach reminded him that he'd had a light lunch. "How about a sandwich to go with our coffee? Looks like they have egg salad and tuna."

"You don't have to—"

"Please. It would be my pleasure."

"I like egg salad," Benny said.

"That's my favorite too." Lucas picked up two sandwiches from the refrigerated case and ordered two black coffees. He remembered that was the way Benny drank his after lunch on Saturday.

Just before he left his apartment, Lucas had opened a box of old photographs he'd brought from Trinity Springs and put a few of his school pictures in his jeans pocket. As soon as he and Benny sat down at the table in the corner, he pulled them out. "I thought you might want to see these." He pushed them across the table.

Benny put down his sandwich and picked up the first one. And then another. He wiped at his face with the back of his hand, and Lucas noticed that a couple of tears had rolled down his cheeks. He continued to study the photos and wipe his eyes, which were now overflowing with emotion. He began to dab with a napkin, but he couldn't stop the flow. It was all Lucas could do to keep from tearing up himself, and he kept swallowing the huge lump that had lodged itself in his throat.

After a few minutes, Benny spoke. "I missed a lot."

"We both did."

"She didn't tell me."

"I know."

"That detective told me she didn't raise you."

"She dropped me off at my grandparents' house on my third birthday. I never heard from her again."

"But now?"

"I've seen her recently. My grandparents have both passed, and I had to find her to probate the will. That's when she told me you didn't know about me."

"It would have… I would have…" His voice caught, and he was incapable of going on.

"I know. It would have made all the difference in the world."

"All the difference." Benny picked up another napkin and continued to wipe tears from his eyes. "I don't usually cry," he said.

"Don't be embarrassed. I've done my share of it since I found out."

"That detective said you've met my father."

"I have. He's the one who told me where I could find you."

"Will you come back and see me again?"

"Of course, I will." They sat in silence for a moment as they ate their sandwiches, and a light switched on in Lucas's head. "But I have a better idea."

"Better?"

"Much better. I have a house in Trinity Springs. It used to belong to my grandparents, but it's mine now. I want to keep it because I like going back on weekends, but it sits empty during the week. I need someone to take care of it for me. Stay in it and tend to minor maintenance issues. Mow the yard. Water the grass and plants when it doesn't rain. Would you be interested?"

"Live there? Leave the street?"

"Yes."

"I don't know."

"It would be a big change, I understand, but I'd like you to meet my friends. Maria lives across the street. You already know her. And my friend Sherise owns the café on the square. And I'll be there on the weekends. There's a bicycle in the garage. You could ride it downtown if you get bored staying in the house."

"I don't have any furniture."

"It's completely furnished."

"I haven't slept in a real bed for over twenty years. Just a cot in a shelter sometimes when it gets really cold."

"You don't have to make a decision now. Just think about it."

Benny nodded. "Can you tell me sometime about your life? Your grandparents that raised you?"

"It would be my pleasure."

Chapter Forty

By the time Lucas left downtown Dallas on his way to Trinity Springs, traffic had picked up, and he had plenty of time creeping along on the freeway to think about his next move. He wanted to see Maria, but Sherise had said he needed to give her a "heads up," so that's what he would do. He activated Bluetooth and called her.

"I'm on my way to Trinity Springs to see you," he said when she answered. "Is this a good time? Are you home?"

"I am. Are you staying at your house all night or going back to Dallas?"

"I'm just driving up for a couple of hours. There's something... Oh, I might as well go ahead and tell you part of it." He couldn't wait until he got to Trinity Springs, so he blurted it out. "I met my father."

"You *did*? You found him already?"

"With a little help. He lives in Dallas. I want to tell you all about it. All about him." *And...I want to see you again. But that's a given these days.*

"Oh, Lucas! That's awesome! I want to hear as soon as possible."

"I should be there in about fifty minutes." Lucas pushed down a little harder on the pedal. "Maybe forty-five. Get ready to be blown away by what you're going to hear."

"Hey," Maria said, "I just had a better idea. Have you ever been to Lenny's Burger Joint just north of Highway 380? I've been craving one of those burgers for a while. Want to meet there so you don't have to drive all the way up? It will give us longer to talk."

And I'll see you sooner. "Sure. That's a great idea. I know where it is and should be there in about twenty minutes."

"It might take me a little longer, but if you get there first, you can order me a sweet tea and a burger with everything but onions. And fries. I'm hungry."

"Deal."

"I can't wait to hear about your father."

"I can't wait to tell you," Lucas said. "You're not going to believe it." *And that's an understatement.*

"This is nice," Maria said as they were digging in to their burgers. "I thought maybe I'd see you last night before you left Trinity Springs."

That was his opening—the one he was hoping for—and he jumped in with both feet. "I was planning to come over, but you had company. There was a white Mercedes parked in front of your house."

"Oh. Right. Well, it's just Monday and I'm seeing you now, so it's all good."

All good? Lucas thought. *Not really. Not until you tell me who he is exactly, what he means to you, and what he was doing at your house last night.*

"So tell me about meeting your father," Maria continued as she added more mustard to her hamburger.

"They never put enough." Apparently the subject of Peter was closed for the evening. But Lucas wasn't about to let it be swept under the rug. Not for long anyway. He had to know.

Maria picked the conversation back up by changing the subject again. "Oh. Before I forget... Paul's taking the group down to Dallas on Saturday, and I'm going to sing again. Would you like to go with us this time? You said you might."

Did she sound nervous, or was he reading too much into it? "Yeah. I'd love to go." *And you have no idea how interesting it will be.*

"Great!" Maria took a long sip of her tea and then laser-focused on Lucas. "Now I want to hear all about your father."

After Lucas had told Maria the unlikely story of Benny, she plied him with question after question.

"Oh, my goodness. This is amazing! And unbelievable! How did he take the news? Did he ask about Carmen? Did he wonder how you found him? I liked him the first time I met him. There's so much more I want to know!"

"It could have gone very differently, but fortunately he's happy I found him. Couldn't believe it at first when Max told him. Very emotional about the time we've lost. I asked him to come to Trinity Springs and live in the house. There's a lot he can do there to help me, and he knows you're just across the street if he needs anything during the week. I'll be home every weekend. I'm looking forward to really getting to know him. Still can't believe the coincidence. Who would have thought one of the guys Paul chose to come to your parents' house was the father I'd been searching for?"

"I believe God puts people and circumstances in our lives for a reason. Maybe Benny's the reason I felt the nudge to come over to your house after not seeing you for so many years. I know that detective would have led you to him anyway, but this way you got to know him a little bit before you both knew about the relationship. Do you think he'll come to Trinity Springs? I hope he does!" Maria put her hands in a position of prayer.

"I didn't want to pressure him, but I told him to think about it and tell me later. There's another reason I'm glad you came over that day, and it has nothing to do with Everett Bennington."

"Oh? Do tell."

"I need to find out something first." This was the moment Lucas had been dreading, but he couldn't let her just drop the subject and move on. He had to know about Peter. Had to know if he still meant something to Maria. He apparently had at one time, but she'd been closed-mouth about it, and the man with the white Mercedes was still a mystery. What happened at her house Sunday night was still a mystery. Lucas had some decisions to make, but he couldn't make them without knowing what was going on.

"Okay."

"I'm talking about the white elephant in the room. Or rather the white Mercedes on the street. I was headed over to your house last night when I saw Peter get out of the car. Later I left the house for a while, and when I came back it was still there. The other night at Oliver's he said he wanted to catch up. You said he was just a friend. I guess what I want to know is this: does he mean something to you? Because if he does, I'll back off. I just want you to be happy. But if he doesn't, well…I'd like to know that too. In case you can't tell, I'm mentally crossing my fingers that it's the latter."

"You deserve to know the whole story, Lucas. Peter is a doctor and in practice with his father, who was our family physician in Dallas. We met when I went in for my yearly exam once, and his father was on vacation. Peter was seeing all of his patients. We started dating shortly after that. Dated for about six months, but when I heard about the music opening at Trinity Springs Elementary, I jumped at the chance to come back. Renters had just moved out of the house on Bailey Street, and that seemed like another sign. At least I took it as a sign because I always loved that house. Good memories might have had a lot to do with it." She smiled at Lucas. "Anyway, a week after I told Peter I was leaving Dallas, he proposed. He led me to believe he would be willing to start a practice in Trinity Springs, so I accepted. More out of thinking it was the obvious next step in our relationship than anything else. I realize now that I didn't love him. It just seemed like the thing to do. You know?"

Lucas dipped a french fry in ketchup, but kept his gaze on Maria. He liked where this seemed to be going and wanted to hear more. Wanted a resolution. "Go on."

"After a few months, I realized he had no intention of leaving Dallas but thought our getting engaged would make me change my mind about taking the new job and moving. So I gave the ring back and told him we had no future. I'm sorry I didn't tell you sooner, but he was out of the picture and doesn't play a role in my life now, so…" She let her voice trail off.

Lucas let out a big sigh of relief and reached for her hand. "You've just made my day. Thanks for filling me in. I'll admit I was a little concerned last night," he said, resisting the urge to say more. Ever since he'd spotted that Mercedes, he'd felt like he was being dragged underwater by a concrete block. But Maria's explanation had put his mind at ease. He believed her. It made sense, and he was able to breathe normally again. He had a strong desire to kiss her, but there would be time later…and in a more romantic setting than a booth in Lenny's Burger Joint.

"You never had any reason to be concerned," she reassured him, "but I understand."

"Oh. One more thing about Benny." Lucas was not only satisfied by what Maria had told him about her brief engagement, but ready to change the subject now too. He'd be happy if he never heard the name Peter again. "Max, the detective who located both him and Carmen, was going to take him a burner phone so he could let me know as soon as he makes a decision about living in Trinity Springs. I'm kind of on pins and needles waiting to hear."

"It might not be an easy decision for him, Lucas. Considering how long he's been living there and the friends he's made. I'm sure Shane would be sad to see him go."

"Yeah. I've thought of that. He'll need time to consider his options, and I need to be patient. I can do that. Hey! It was a good idea...meeting in the middle like this. Thanks for saving me an hour of driving."

"You have put a few miles on your car lately."

"It's been worth it. But I guess I'd better head back. Got a busy week ahead of me at work."

Lucas walked Maria to her car, pulled her close and kissed her, gently at first, but then more passionately, his hands caressing the curve of her back. "I wish... Never mind. I might have something to tell you next time I see you."

"That's cruel."

"I know. Sorry. The weekend will be here before you know it, though."

Chapter Forty-One

Lucas had been wrong. Monday evening to Friday seemed like an eternity to Maria. But she busied herself with school and even drove out to Cypress Grove Wednesday after the three o'clock bell rang. She hadn't heard from Lucas and assumed he hadn't heard from Benny or he would have called. He'd given her the go-ahead to tell her parents and Paul about locating his father. She'd called Paul to relay the news but wanted to tell her parents in person.

"We had no idea Lucas knew the name of his father," Livvy said as they sat around the kitchen table finishing a meal of fried chicken and all the trimmings. "I wonder why Carmen listed him on the birth certificate if she left without telling him she was pregnant."

"I don't know, but I'm glad she did." Maria took another drumstick off the platter. "Lucas deserves to know where he came from. And now he and his father can have a relationship. That's my hope, at least. He asked Benny to live in the house on Bailey Street and help him take care of it. He's thinking about it."

"Another fishing buddy!" Rob exclaimed. "I think he enjoyed it when he was here."

"We need to tread softly and slowly, Daddy. Remember he's been on the street for a very long time. It could be quite an adjustment to completely change everything he's used to all at once. Of course, we're assuming he's going to say yes."

"Why wouldn't he?" Rob asked. "A chance to get in out of the elements? Extreme heat and extreme cold. Who wouldn't jump at that offer?"

"Are you forgetting he left the home of one of the wealthiest families in Dallas to live on the street? And we're not completely sure what prompted that. By the way, don't tell anyone else about this. We need to protect the family. Benny's mother and brother don't know he's been located," Maria said. "It's Thomas Bennington's decision when and how to tell them. Unfortunately, it will probably hit the papers at some point. They're such a well known and established family in Dallas."

"I'm sure a lot of healing needs to take place, but Benny has a son now," Livvy offered. "That has to count for something."

"I hope so," Maria said. "Lucas said he seemed happy to meet him but sad about the lost years."

"Lost years," Livvy echoed. "That has to hurt."

Maria nodded. "Benny is such a sweet guy. I knew that the first day I met him. Lucas is going with us Saturday. I hope he gets an answer then."

"I'm not one to say 'I told you so,' but remember when I encouraged you to give Lucas a chance about the homeless situation? I had a feeling he'd come around. He was raised right, and I knew you two could meet in the middle about that situation."

"I'm just glad he was coming around, as you say, before he knew Benny was his father. I think that says a lot about him. He knows about Peter now too. We talked it out Monday. I told him everything, which I should have done sooner. You were right again, Mama, but he's okay with it. Things are good with us."

Rob quit eating, laid down his fork, and looked at his daughter. "*How* good? A dad needs to know these things."

"Daddy! You don't have to worry about anything. Lucas is a gentleman, and right now we're just friends. Well, sort of..." She smiled across the table at him, thankful to know her father would do anything for her but wouldn't interfere in her affairs without an invitation.

"Yeah. It's that 'sort of' that concerns me." He winked. "Just kidding. You know I like that boy."

"I'm glad. He feels the same way about y'all. Let me help you clean up the kitchen, Mama. Then I'd better get back."

"You go ahead before it gets dark," Rob said. "I'll help your mother with the dishes."

At nine o'clock on Saturday morning, Lucas arrived on Maria's front porch with the most beautiful bouquet of spring flowers she'd ever seen. It was a particularly warm day in May, and they were driving to Dallas in his car rather than the church van in case Benny was ready to pack up his belongings and come back to Trinity Springs with them. Lucas had spent Friday evening getting the house ready, just in case. Maria had offered to make scrambled eggs for breakfast before they headed out for what could possibly be a very eventful day for both Benny and his newly discovered son.

"Ooh! Gorgeous," Maria said when she opened the door and saw the flowers. "What's the occasion?"

"Just because. I thought they were beautiful, and you're beautiful, so..."

She wrapped her arms around his neck. "Thank you. I love that you didn't have to have a special occasion to give me flowers. But it's a special day anyway. I'm so excited to see if Benny has made a decision yet."

Lucas kissed her on the forehead. "I hope he's decided to come, but let's don't get our hopes up. It might take him a while to make that decision. It would be a big change for him."

"Huge."

"Do you have a vase? I couldn't find one at home."

"Sure. I'll take care of those while you check the oven to see if the biscuits are done." Maria constantly marveled now at Lucas's change of attitude. Only a few weeks ago, she wouldn't have dreamed of asking him to go to Dallas with her and the church group because she knew he'd make some excuse for not being able to go. And she was thankful he'd done an about-face before he knew Benny was his father. She could tell he hadn't minded being with Benny and Shane at her parents' house. In fact, he seemed to enjoy them and appreciate the fact that they had served in the military. They'd earned his respect then, and now he was inviting one to live in his house. Such a whirlwind of events in only a few days, but Maria was thrilled.

They were almost finished with their eggs and biscuits when she remembered something Lucas had said when they were at Lenny's Monday night. "You said you might have something to tell me the next time we were together. Do you?"

"As a matter of fact, I do. But I'm going to wait until we're back home tonight. We don't have time to go into it now. What time do we need to be there?"

"Around eleven, give or take a few minutes, so I guess we'd better go soon. But I'm not going to let you forget you're supposed to tell me something."

"You don't have to worry about that. It's not a matter I could forget."

"You do know how to pique my curiosity."

"I like to keep you wondering. That way I know you're thinking about me," Lucas said with a wink as he started clearing the table.

Chapter Forty-Two

Lucas and Maria arrived at their destination at ten after eleven, and the group from Trinity Springs Bible Fellowship were already there. Shane and Benny were helping Paul and the others from church set up tables. A crowd had started to gather, and an older stooped-over man with several teeth missing asked Benny, "That your son?"

Benny nodded.

Without hesitation, Lucas stepped over to the man and held out his hand. "I'm Lucas Avila, and Benny is my father. What's your name?"

The man took Lucas's hand and tried to straighten his body and look him in the eye. "I'm Raymond, sir. Benny's right proud of you."

"Pleased to meet you. I'm proud of him too," Lucas said, trying to keep his voice even. "He was in the army, you know. Fought in Desert Storm. Shane too. And I imagine I'll meet more veterans here."

"I was in Vietnam '70 and '71."

"Then I'm doubly pleased to meet you," Lucas said. "Thank you for your service." He looked back at Maria, who was standing with eyes wide and mouth agape. "I guess I'd better help with the food," he told Raymond and started toward her. She met him halfway.

"You're amazing. You know that?"

"No, I'm not. I think I just woke up. Let's go say hi to Benny."

Lucas was trying desperately not to get his hopes built up about his father's decision, but it just wasn't happening. He couldn't keep his anticipation from bubbling over. When he glanced at Maria, he was sure she could see it. But he knew she hoped Benny would move too, because she'd been drawn to him from the first time she'd met him and heard him sing. Lucas remembered she'd mentioned his military service and called him impressive.

"Have you been thinking about living in Trinity Springs, Benny?" Lucas asked.

"Would it help you?"

"It would. There's a lot you could do, and I would be home every weekend. I'd like to get to know you after all the time we've lost."

"I really wish she had... Oh, well... We can't change the past. Could I... Would someone bring me back sometime to see my friends? Shane thinks I should go. He said Willie would watch his stuff when he goes to the library, but I don't know. These are my people. They have been for a long time."

"I'll bring you back. And Paul will, I'm sure. And Shane can come to Trinity Springs for visits too."

Paul ambled over to where the three of them were standing. "Did I hear my name?"

"Paul," Lucas said, "you know I've invited Benny to come to Trinity Springs and live in my house on Bailey Street."

"So I heard." Paul smiled at Benny and arched his eyebrows in a questioning look.

"He's concerned about missing his friends," Lucas said. "I can understand that, but I assured him you and I will bring him back to see them."

"Of course we will. Benny, you can be my point man with this ministry. Who knows it better than you? You know I bring some folks down almost every weekend. I might ask you to head up the team. You know what people need. You can help me collect and distribute coats and blankets for the winter. We'd be lucky to have someone with your expertise on the team."

"So I could help Lucas *and* you?" Benny asked and Paul nodded.

"And my daddy," Maria added. "He'd love to have a fishing buddy close by."

"What about a trial period? Two weeks? And if it isn't working out..." Benny suggested.

"That's fine. We don't want you to feel pressured. You've been here a long time. It will be an adjustment, but I think you'll feel at home there in no time," Lucas assured him.

"Is there a library?"

"Yes! The library is a twenty-minute walk or a ten-minute bike ride from the house. It's small, but I think you'll like it."

"Okay. I'll go. But not today. I have to tell someone goodbye next week."

Lucas put his hand on his father's shoulder. "I'm so glad. What if I pick you up on Friday afternoon when I get off work? Around six?" *We might not have the past, but we have the future.*

After the food had been devoured, tables cleared, and Paul had given a five-minute talk about forgiveness, Maria perched herself and her guitar on the stool for a few songs. She sang "Because He Lives" and "I Can Only Imagine" and then asked for requests. "Lucas and I need to leave by one-thirty, but we have time for a couple more songs. I know some of you have favorites you'd like to hear. They don't have to be gospel songs."

Benny raised his hand, and Shane hollered out, "Miss Maria, Benny has a new song now!"

"Great! What would you like to hear, Benny?"

"Do you know any Willie Nelson?" he asked.

"Well, I'd better or I might lose my Texas citizenship, right?" Laughter trickled through the crowd. "What are you thinking about?"

"Do you know 'Blue Skies'?"

"Sure! That's a great Irving Berlin song, and I love the way Willie sings it. Will you help me?"

He nodded.

Maria played an introduction and opened her mouth to sing, but her voice caught. Emotion clogged her throat. No words came out. No sound. Nothing. A couple of tears escaped her eyes and rolled down her cheeks, but she kept on playing and Benny started singing on the second line. Lucas walked over, put his arm around his father, and joined him on the third line.

"I'm sorry," she said when the song was over. "I guess I'm just a little emotional today. But you guys sounded really good together. I'll see you all again soon." She hopped down from the stool and put her guitar in its case. No more songs today. Nothing could top what had just happened.

Summer was advancing on Trinity Springs and the afternoon was warm when choir practice was over at four o'clock and Maria got in her blue Chevy and headed for home. All the way back from Dallas and during choir practice she'd tried to imagine what Lucas was planning to tell her. They'd made a date to have dinner and watch a movie at her house at six, and that would give her plenty of time to get ready. Fortunately, she didn't have to cook. Lucas was picking up Chinese.

She felt their relationship was on the verge of something, but she couldn't quite put her finger on it. The butterflies in her stomach spoke not of nervousness, but rather excitement. Things had been going so well with them lately, and today he'd shown his character, when dealing with Raymond especially. It was one thing to feel comfortable with Shane and Benny. He'd been with them before. But quite another when he talked to a homeless man he'd never met...and with the courtesy he extended to the man. Lucas had been on a remarkable journey, and Maria felt blessed to have been there to witness it.

When the doorbell rang, Maria ran her brush through her hair one more time, took a deep breath, and ran to answer the door. Her anticipation was almost off the charts. What was it he was going to tell her that had to wait this long?

She opened the door to the guy she'd had a crush on for more than twenty years. When she was in high school, she'd imagine she and Lucas still lived in the same town and he invited her to the prom. When she was in school musicals, she pretended he was in the audience, glowing with pride. When she was maid-of-honor in her best friend's wedding, he was the best man and they were dancing together at the reception.

But it was real now. This handsome guy standing on her porch holding bags filled with boxes of Chinese food was real, and she was smitten.

"I hope," he said when she opened the door, "you don't get tired of me today. This is, after all, our third meal together today."

"Trust me. I'm not tired of you. And I won't get tired of you." *Understatement of the century*, Maria thought.

"Well, that's good, in light of what I'm going to tell you tonight. Can we talk about it after we eat, though? I've been smelling this food all the way from Chang's, and I'm starving."

"Sure." *I feel as though I've already waited an eternity, but I guess I can wait a little longer.* "Let me pour us some tea. I've been wondering all day what it could be."

They ate their cashew chicken in almost complete silence, but breaking the silence every few minutes with something mundane like *How was your week at work?* and *It's already hot for this time of year, isn't it?*

When they'd finished their meal and the kitchen was completely cleaned up, Lucas suggested they move to the living room. Maria sat down on the sofa first. He joined her, scooted a little closer, and took her hand in his.

"I think I know the answer to this," he started. "I hope I know the answer to this. But I was wondering if you'd be upset if I move back to Trinity Springs and open a law practice on the square."

"Upset? What's the opposite of upset?" A huge smile appeared on her face.

"Joyful comes to mind," he offered, with that crooked grin she thought she could spend a lifetime feasting her eyes on.

"You're serious, right? Because if you're not, I *will* be upset. Don't play with my emotions, Lucas."

"I'm dead serious. I didn't want to mention it to you until I'd made a firm decision, but I put a down payment on office space around the corner from Sherise's while you were in choir practice this afternoon."

"That's a huge step. Are you sure? I'm not trying to talk you out of it. Of course, I'm thrilled. I just don't want you to regret giving up a sure thing and starting over."

"I've been thinking about it for a while. I'm ready to leave corporate law, and I know I could pull business from neighboring towns…wills, estates, divorces, custody, property settlements, contracts. I've done a little research, and most of them don't have a local attorney. The first thing that spurred me to go ahead with the decision was when I saw the For Lease sign in the window of the office space on the square. The second was when I called Thomas Bennington this afternoon to tell him about Benny's decision. He was overjoyed his son will be off the street. I can't remember if I told you, but when I first met him, he offered to give me $50,000 every year to quit looking for Everett. Wanted me to just drop it and not tell anyone. I would have had to sign a nondisclosure agreement to continue getting the money. I refused, but instead of getting mad, he was impressed that I couldn't be bought off. So when I told him Benny was coming to live in my house, he brought up the money again. I think he's trying to make things even for his two sons. What he hasn't been able to do for Everett all these years…he sees the opportunity to do now, through me. But he doesn't want Benny to know. Pride and all. Told me he won't take no for an answer. I'd already made the decision, but that phone call tied it up with a neat bow."

She'd listened, her eyes never leaving Lucas's face, but she hadn't heard what she wanted desperately to hear.

"Oh," he said, winking and gathering her into his arms, "did I forget to mention the main reason I'm moving home? I love being on the street where you live." He stopped talking long enough to kiss her. "'On the Street Where You Live.' Catchy title for a song. Someone should write it."

There it was. He'd said it, and she was overjoyed. "I *really* like your main reason. Did I ever tell you I played Eliza in *My Fair Lady* when I was a senior in high school?"

"I'll bet you were great in that role. Would I lose my man card if I confessed to liking that movie…a lot?"

"Lose it? You'd get a gold star on your man card for that revelation. I have it DVR'd…and…we were wondering what to watch tonight. So…?"

"I vote for it. It's three hours instead of two. Longer to be with you." He pushed back a strand of her dark brown hair that had fallen across her eye.

"I'm so glad you're coming home, Lucas."

"I *am* coming home. But home is not a place. It's a person. And you're my person." He kissed her a long, perfect kiss, and her heart was full.

About the Author

Rebecca Stevenson is a native Texan, but marriage took her to New England and the Maine coast stole her heart. She lives in Texas again, but frequent trips back to the Northeast were the inspirations and settings for her Wentworth Cove series.

New Song: A Trinity Springs Novel is the first book in a new series set in her home state of Texas.

A former English and creative writing teacher, she thought if she could teach writing, she should be able to do it. Those thoughts and some brainstorming sessions with her daughter led to her first novel, *Another Summer*, set in a picturesque coastal village in Maine. From that debut novel, the Wentworth Cove series was born.

Her greatest blessings are her family, friends, and faithful canine companion, Baxter. Long walks and dark chocolate are her muses.

She's currently working on the second book in the Trinity Springs series, *Skye Blue*, which will be out in the fall of 2023.

Made in the USA
Coppell, TX
26 December 2022